LEN HAMILTON 34

DR

PAUL TEMPLE
And
THE MADISON CASE

Francis Durbridge

PAUL TEMPLE

And

THE MADISON CASE

Hodder & Stoughton

LONDON SYDNEY AUCKLAND TORONTO

British Library Cataloguing in Publication Data

Francis Durbridge
  Paul temple and the madison case.
  I. Title
  823'.914[F]   PR6063.A167

  ISBN 0 340 41608 4

First published 1988

Published by Hodder and Stoughton,
a division of Hodder and Stoughton Ltd,
Mill Road, Dunton Green, Sevenoaks, Kent TN13 2YE
Editorial Office: 47 Bedford Square, London WC1B 3DP

Photoset by Chippendale Type
Otley, West Yorkshire

Printed in Great Britain by St Edmundsbury Press Ltd,
Bury St Edmunds, Suffolk

Contents

1   My Name is Portland, Sam Portland

"I think I'll go up on deck for a few minutes, Paul. I'd like to take a last look at the New York skyline."

"Isn't it a bit late, Steve? You said you wanted to change your dress before going down to dinner."

"Yes, I know, but it will clear my head a bit."

"You're not feeling off colour already, are you? It's only ten minutes since we sailed."

"No, darling, I'm fine. It's just that I feel a little sea air will do me good."

"Well, take a wrap or something. And for heaven's sake don't get lost. Do you know the number of this cabin?"

"I know we're on the Signal Deck and isn't it eight hundred and something?"

"We're on the Sports Deck and it's number 8020."

Mr and Mrs Paul Temple were on their way back from a stay in New York. They had flown out by Concorde and were returning in more leisurely fashion on the newly refurbished *Princess Diana*. Temple had been attending the International Conference of Anti-Crime Agencies. As an eminent criminologist as well as an author of world renown, he had been invited to deliver the key-note address. His New York publishers had timed the publication of his new book to coincide with the conference and had offered to pay both his and Steve's expenses. After a week of lectures and seminars, interspersed with book signings and television interviews, he was looking forward to five days crossing the Atlantic at 29 knots instead of the Mach 2 of Concorde.

Steve had not been telling the complete truth when she said she was feeling fine. She was a bad sailor and whenever she boarded a ship and knew that she had left terra firma she began to feel queasy. Even on this huge liner, the length of three football pitches, she had a sense of being somehow trapped and enclosed.

As always, coming out on deck made things better. She

was glad that she had not missed this magical moment. The great liner, dwarfed by the soaring skyscrapers on Manhattan Island, was just passing between the upraised arm of the Statue of Liberty and the twin towers of the World Trade Centre. Already the city was beginning to sparkle as lights were switched on in offices where staff would be working till the small hours. She tried to pick out the Waldorf Astoria in the closely packed muddle of buildings. The hotel had been their home for the last six days.

"Isn't that just the most fantastic skyline?"

Steve did not turn round at once. The voice was American but she was not sure whether the remark had been addressed to her. She was adept at dealing with approaches from strangers who could not resist the lure of an attractive woman on her own.

"The Big Apple. It's a sight that always brings a lump into my throat."

Steve turned. The man leaning on the rail beside her was wearing a white suit and a gaily coloured tie. His hair was grey and thinning on top, but she did not put him at much more than fifty. His colour was high but whether from recent sunshine or blood pressure she could not tell. There was an unmistakable air of prosperity about him and she guessed that his corpulent build was a consequence of good living.

"I was just trying to make out the Waldorf Astoria. That's where my husband and I stayed."

"Say, you're English! I just love that accent. How long you been over here?"

"Only a week. We flew over on Concorde but decided to make a holiday of the return journey."

"You're dead right. No better way to spend five days than in a ship like this."

The American leant a hand against the rail and stared up at the single red smoke stack. The wisp of pale blue vapour from the three diesel turbines was tugged westwards by the fresh sea breeze.

"It's funny," Steve said. "I can't see the Empire State Building."

"I guess it just slipped behind the World Trade Centre. You'll see it in a minute. You spend your week in New York?"

"Most of it. My husband was attending the ICACA conference."

His expression had not changed at these mentions of a husband.

"How did you like it?"

"New York? I liked it enormously."

"It's some city, isn't it?" He gave her an infectious grin. "You know, I've heard a lot of English people say they wouldn't like to live in New York, but I just can't imagine why they say that. It's got everything."

"That's probably why they wouldn't like to live there."

"Yeah?" His voice had become a little suspicious, wary. "That's too subtle for me."

"Is this your first trip to England?" Steve asked, deciding to keep the conversation on more conventional lines.

"M'm-m'm, I guess it is." He nodded then added seriously, "At least I don't think I've been there before."

"You don't think . . . ?" Steve laughed, taking it as a joke. "Don't you know?"

"Well, you see, I only . . . " He hesitated, then abruptly his manner changed. He held out his hand. "Maybe we ought to introduce ourselves. My name is Portland, Sam Portland."

Steve took the proffered hand, which grasped hers strongly.

"I'm Mrs Temple."

"Was that your husband I saw you with – the tall, tired-looking gentleman?"

"Yes, that was my husband."

Sam Portland was looking at her with renewed interest. "I've read quite a lot about your husband, Mrs Temple, but somehow I never imagined he looked like that."

"Confidentially he doesn't." Steve smiled. "He's suffering from an overdose of American hospitality."

"Oh, so that's it," Portland said with a conspiratorial chuckle.

"He'll look quite different tomorrow." Steve assured him.

"Maybe we'll all look different tomorrow."

"Why, is it going to be rough?"

Hearing Steve's tone of alarm Portland put his hands up, palm towards her. "No, no! Aren't you a good sailor?"

"Not very," Steve admitted.

"Well that's O.K. I'll fix it," Portland promised with a

twinkle. "I'll have a word with the Captain. Don't worry Mrs Temple, it'll be as smooth as a glass of milk." Then he added, as an afterthought, "I hope."

"Look!" Steve exclaimed. "There's the Empire State coming into view now."

As if to salute it, the *Princess Diana* gave two blasts of her horn. A few seconds later a multiple echo came back across the water from the impressive skyscrapers. Steve shivered and pulled the shawl tighter round her shoulders.

Thanks to the generosity of the American publishers the Temples had one of the special state rooms on the topmost deck of the liner. The suite consisted of a bedroom with bathroom en suite and a luxuriously appointed sitting room with VCR, TV, compact disc and radio plus a direct dial satellite telephone. A door gave access to their private verandah on the starboard side.

Temple was tying his bow tie in the bedroom mirror. Two cocktail glasses, delivered by room service, stood on the low table.

"I ordered your usual dry Martini, darling. I hope that's right."

"Perfect." Steve slid open the door of the long wardrobe where her dresses had been hung. "Now, what shall I wear?"

"What about that Yuki you bought at Bloomingdale's?"

"No, I think I'll keep that for the last night."

Steve selected a dress, laid it on the bed and began to take off her tights.

"Paul, have you ever heard of a man called Sam Portland?"

"Sam Portland? Good lord yes! Why?"

"He's on board. I've just been having a chat with him."

"You've heard of Sam Portland. Portland's Yeast . . . It's all over America."

"Oh, is that him?"

"Yes, that's Mr Portland all right. What's he like?"

"I rather liked him, but . . . "

Temple gave his bow a final tweak and turned. "But what?"

"He said rather a peculiar thing, darling. I asked him if he'd ever been to England before and he said, 'No, I don't think so'."

"He doesn't think so? Surely he knows whether he's been to England or not! He was pulling your leg."

"No, he wasn't." Steve threw her discarded tights onto a chair. "He was serious."

"Must have been pulling your leg."

"Paul, he wasn't," she insisted. "I simply asked him whether he'd ever been . . . "

"Steve, for goodness sake stop arguing and get dressed, otherwise we'll be late for dinner."

Steve stood up and put a hand on the back of the chair.

"Oh dear . . ."

"What's the matter?"

"The cabin's swaying . . . I hope it's not going to be rough . . . "

"You're imagining things. We're only just passing Ellis Island."

Room service had brought the Temples breakfast in bed, served on two trays with short legs. The lavish spread was entirely wasted on Steve, who could only nibble a piece of toast and sip a cup of coffee. Temple had got up and dressed soon afterwards and taken the lift down to the Promenade Deck. He wanted to get some exercise and had made three circuits of the ship before he paused, leaning on the rail and looking out over the bows. The ship was sailing at her cruising speed of 29 knots.

It was a fine, sunny day and the sea was calm. America had long since slipped down over the horizon, somewhere beyond the straight white wake churned up by the twelve blades of the twin propellers.

"Excuse me, sir . . . Mr Temple?"

Warily Temple turned to look at the man who had come up to lean on the rail beside him.

"Yes?"

"My name is Portland."

Temple's face relaxed into a warm smile. "Oh, good morning, Mr Portland."

"I had the pleasure of meeting your wife last night, Mr Temple . . . "

"Yes, so she told me."

"I was wondering how the little lady was feeling this morning."

11

"She's not too good, I'm afraid."

"On a diet?" Sam Portland suggested tactfully.

"Strictly on a diet," Temple replied with a straight face.

"Well now, that's too bad. If there's anything I can do for Mrs Temple, please let me know."

"That's very kind of you."

A little posse of youngsters in jogging gear trotted past, laughing and joking amongst themselves. Temple pointed to the deck chairs which had been set out by the crew.

"Won't you sit down?"

"Why thank you, sir!" Sam Portland lowered himself carefully into a chair and held up his large half-smoked cigar. "Does my smoking bother you?"

"Not at all."

"Would you like a cigar?"

"Thank you, not at the moment."

The American drew thoughtfully on his Havana cigar. "Mr Temple, I was very thrilled when I saw your name on the passenger list last night."

"Indeed?"

"I've been an admirer of yours for some considerable time. As a matter of fact I once wrote you a letter."

"I can't recall ever having received a letter from you, Mr Portland."

"No, you didn't receive it, for the simple reason that I didn't post it." Portland chuckled. "My wife persuaded me to change my mind."

"I see," Temple said, somewhat mystified.

"Mr Temple, forgive me talking shop at this time of the morning but have you heard of a private investigator – a detective – by the name of Madison?"

"Madison? No."

"I rather imagine he's pretty well known in your country."

"Well, he can't be very well known or I should have heard of him."

"Are you sure you haven't? Madison." Portland spelt the name out letter by letter.

"Quite sure."

"Well, now that's very curious." Portland shrugged "Still, why should I worry if he gets the results."

"Is he working for you?"

"Er-yes. Actually he's employed by my London representative, a man called Hubert Greene."

"What is Madison doing exactly?"

"He's on a research job."

"Sales? Statistics?" Temple prompted.

Portland paused, then said slowly "No, no, no, nothing
like that. Purely a private investigation. *He's trying to find out
who I am.*"

Temple stared at him. "Who you are?"

"Yes," said Portland, nodding.

"But you know who you are! You're Sam Portland."

"Sure. Sure, I'm Sam Portland. Samuel L. Portland,
President of the Portland Yeast Company. New York,
Chicago, Detroit, Michigan and all points west. I'm one of
the wealthiest men in America, Mr Temple, did you know
that?"

Temple laughed. "I had a shrewd suspicion."

"Right now I could lay my hands on four hundred million
dollars. It's an awful lot of dough."

"It's an awful lot of dough, Mr Portland." Temple agreed
seriously. He drew his legs in as another group of joggers,
more elderly ones this time, ambled past.

"Four hundred million bucks and I don't know who I am!
Mr Temple, would you like to hear my story?"

Too late Temple was regretting the encouragement he
had given the American.

"Well, as a matter of fact I did promise my wife . . . "

"You're going to hear it anyway, so you might just as well
relax!"

Temple echoed Portland's laugh. The American leant on
the arm of his chair and spoke in a confidential tone.

"Thirty-five years ago, on October 9th 1952 to be precise,
a Chicago policeman by the name of Dan Kelly arrested a
young man for jay walking – you know what I mean, trying
to beat the traffic. The young fella turned out to be
something of a problem. He was suffering from what the
doctors called amnesia, or to put it bluntly, just plain loss of
memory."

Portland waited for a couple who had paused in front of
them to move on.

"Go on . . . " said Temple, intrigued in spite of himself.

"The young man was acquitted and the policeman – Kelly

13

— took him under his wing. Kelly was convinced that sooner or later the young man's memory would return, Mr Temple, but the young fella never established his true identity."

Portland's cigar had gone out. He gave it an accusing look then laid it on the deck beside his chair.

"Go on, Mr Portland."

"I lived with Kelly for the best part of seven years. We got along famously together. I guess he was like a father and the proverbial big brother rolled into one. In 1958 I moved to New York and started the Portland Yeast Company. The rest you can guess. It was just a long, long trail leading to four hundred million dollars."

"What made you choose the name Portland?"

"Well, I had to call myself something." Portland laughed and a gold tooth flashed. "I was on Portland Avenue when Kelly arrested me."

"But couldn't you remember anything?"

"Not a thing."

"Hadn't you any marks of identification?"

"No. When I was arrested I had three dollars in my pocket, a white handkerchief, a fountain pen and curiously enough an English penny."

"An English penny?"

"Yes. I've still got it. Look, it's on my watch-chain."

Portland was wearing a waistcoat. Temple wondered if he did so purely in order to accommodate a gold watch and chain. He inserted two fingers in the left-hand pocket and withdrew one of the big old-fashioned pennies. The copper glittered in the morning sunlight. Either it had been treated with some lacquer or he polished it every day. Temple leant over to study it but Portland had quickly slipped the coin back into his pocket.

"How does this fellow Madison fit into the picture?"

"I'll tell you." He hitched himself round in his chair to face Temple more squarely. "For years now I've been making inquiries in the hope of finding things out about myself. If you were in my shoes wouldn't you want to know who your parents were, where you came from and why on a certain afternoon in the year 1952 you were suddenly discovered wandering down Portland Avenue in Chicago?

Well, two weeks ago Hubert Greene, my London representative, 'phoned through to New York. He told me that a man
called Madison – a well known private inquiry agent in
London – had discovered certain facts concerning my
identity. As you can imagine this sort of thing wasn't exactly
new to me so I told Hubert to look into the matter."

"Did he?"

"Yes he did. Three days ago he telexed me. He said he
was convinced that Madison was on the level."

Portland leant forward and gripped the arms of his deck
chair. "I'm finding this sea breeze a little too healthy for my
liking. What do you say we move into the Midships Lounge?
I hear they serve a very good hot bouillon there at eleven
o'clock."

The two men stood up and began to stroll down the
starboard side of the ship.

"Frankly," said Portland, "I was rather surprised just now
when you told me that you'd never heard of Madison."

"Well, I can soon check on him for you. I've got some very
good friends at Scotland Yard."

"I hope that won't be necessary, but if it is I'll let you
know." Portland laid a hand on Temple's arm. "Oh, by the
way, if you happen to meet Mrs Portland don't mention this
Madison story. She doesn't know anything about it."

"No?"

"No, you see my wife takes the attitude that I should let
the past take care of itself. 'Why should you worry, Sam,'
she says, 'you're sitting pretty anyway.'"

"Well, that's certainly a point of view," said Temple,
laughing. "Is your wife an American, Mr Portland?"

"No, she's English although she's lived in America for a
great many years. As a matter of fact we've only been
married six weeks."

"Oh!" Temple quickly controlled his surprise. "Congratulations!"

"Thanks," said Sam, accepting the congratulations with
the satisfied expression of a cat that had scooped the milk.

"Why are you making this trip – for business reasons or
simply to meet Madison?"

"Well, my wife thinks I'm making it because of Moira.
Oh, Moira's my daughter – by my first marriage, of course.
She works in my London office. Actually, however, I must

confess I'm coming over simply because of Madison. I'm sold on Madison, Temple. I really think he's found something. Hello, here's George." Portland had spotted a man pushing his way towards them beckoning excitedly with one arm. "Now what does he want?"

Temple estimated George Kelly's age as about forty. He was wearing sneakers, jeans and a brightly coloured sports blouse. All in all he seemed an unlikely appendage for the multi-millionaire.

"There's been a 'phone call from the New York office," he announced excitedly. "I couldn't find you so I told 'em you'd ring back. They seemed to be all steamed up about something."

"Yes, all right, George." Sam answered him with an almost fatherly pat on the shoulder. "How's Mrs Portland?"

"About the same. She don't look too good." Kelly's high-pitched laugh twisted his thin mouth. "I reckon she don't feel too good either."

"O.K. I'll be right down."

Kelly nodded, glanced at Temple, then departed.

"That's George Kelly." Sam was watching the man's receding back thoughtfully. "When poor old Dan died I promised to find his son a job. He's my secretary. I guess you wouldn't think so though to hear him talk. George is a drip! He hasn't got the old man's guts, personality or anything else. Still, what can you do?" He shrugged resignedly. "Well, I'll go down and see how my good lady's getting on. Nice to have met you, Mr Temple," offering his hand. "Let's all have a drink together sometime."

."Yes, let's do that."

"Say we meet in the Princess Bar at seven o'clock? I'll bring Mrs Portland along. How's that?"

"Fine."

"And don't forget to bring Mrs Temple."

"Well," said Temple, laughing. "I will if she can make it."

"She'll make it all right."

Sam was lighting another cigar as he moved away in the wake of George Kelly. Temple gave him a minute's start then made his own way to the door that led to the Midships Lounge. He was less interested in the bouillon than in locating the ship's Business Centre with it's Telex, Fax, up-to-date financial reports and secretarial facilities.

The Princess Bar, adjoining the Princess grille, was on the Boat Deck, conveniently placed for the occupants of the prestigious suites just aft of the signals and communications tower. By seven o'clock it was already well filled and virtually everybody there had already changed into evening dress. The sun was sinking towards the horizon and the orange glow of its reflection on the sea cast a warm light on the ceiling of the bar. There was little movement on the well-stabilised ship. The tremor of the nine diesel engines in the belly of the liner was hardly detectable. Already they had thrust *Princess Diana* seven hundred miles out into the Atlantic.

Temple was shepherding Steve towards an empty table by the window. She was walking gingerly, not too sure of her sea legs. More than one pair of eyes rested on them with frank appraisal. They were a striking couple. With his tall build, clean-cut features and the confidence with which he wore his London tailored clothes, Temple looked as British as the ship they were travelling on. Steve always turned heads, for she kept her figure in marvellous trim.

"Are you feeling all right, Steve?"

"Yes, I'm all right now, Paul."

"You certainly look better than you did this morning."

"I certainly feel better!"

They settled into low armchairs facing the colourful gathering. At once a waiter in the ship's grey and green livery materialised before them.

"What can I get you, madam?"

"What would you like, darling?" Temple enquired. "Have a champagne cocktail."

"Is that a good idea?" She looked at her husband doubtfully.

"It's a very good idea. Two champagne cocktails."

"Yes, sir."

The waiter hurried towards the bar. Steve's eyes were checking over the men in their black and white tuxedos.

"I don't see Mr Portland."

"No, he hasn't arrived yet." Temple had hardly spoken when he saw George Kelly coming in with a woman. The secretary's wiry body had been crammed uncomfortably into a black jacket and trousers. He and his companion were

17

ill-matched. She was a good looking blonde in her forties, with a generous, full figure and slightly florid face. Her dress was obviously a model from a top designer. "But here's his secretary!"

"Who's he with?"

"I don't know, unless it's Mrs Portland."

"She's not that young, surely."

George Kelly quickly spotted Temple. He pushed his way through the tables, clearing a passage for Stella Portland.

"Excuse me, Mr Temple. Have you seen Mr Portland?"

"No." Temple had stood in expectation of being introduced to the lady. "We arranged to meet here at seven o'clock but I am afraid he hasn't shown up yet."

"I'm beginning to feel very worried, George." said Stella, biting her lip.

"There's nothing to worry about," Kelly reassured her. He added with his cracked laugh, "He's probably found a quiet corner somewhere and fallen asleep."

Stella shook her head. "That's not like Sam. He doesn't do that sort of thing." Then she turned her baby-blue eyes on Temple. "Are you Mr Temple?"

"Yes."

"I'm Stella Portland," she said, holding out her hand.

"I'm glad to meet you, Mrs Portland." Temple took the hand which was held for a moment in her warm grasp. "This is my wife . . . "

"How do you do, Mrs Temple?" Wisely, Steve did not stand up. "I hope you're feeling better now, my husband told me that you were not too good this morning."

"I'm much better, thank you."

"Seasickness must be really dreadful," Stella said, with earnest sympathy. "I always feel frightfully sorry for anyone who suffers from it. Fortunately, I'm a very good sailor." She turned to the secretary who was staring at Steve with undisguised admiration. "George, I do wish you'd go and look for Sam. I'm really dreadfully worried."

"O.K." Kelly was reluctant to be banished from the party. "O.K., Stella!"

With unconcealed ill-humour the secretary departed, fidgeting his shoulders in his jacket.

"I don't know what's happened to Sam." Stella was too

worried to take one of the vacant chairs. "No one seems to have seen him since lunch time."

"Have you looked in the gymnasium?" Temple too had remained standing.

"My husband's hardly the sort of man to spend an afternoon in the gymnasium."

Her tone was sharp but Temple put it down to tension.

"Well, what would you like to drink, Mrs Portland?"

"May I have a scotch? On the rocks."

"Yes of course."

Temple was trying to attract the attention of the waiter when one of the ship's officers came into the bar. He had his cap under his arm and his sleeve was braided with gold. His eyes searched the assembly and quickly spotted Mrs Portland and Temple. Her back was turned and she did not see him approaching.

"Paul!" said Steve, *sotto voce*. "This must be the Captain and he's coming to talk to us!"

"That's not the Captain, darling. It's the Purser."

"Excuse me, sir." The Purser already knew Temple, as he had prevented a television crew from filming his arrival on the ship. He turned to Stella. His face was grave. "Mrs Portland?"

"Yes." Stella had paled. She already sensed that something was wrong.

"The ship's doctor would like to see you in the Health Centre, Mrs Portland."

"To see me?"

"Yes."

"But why should I — ? What is it? What has happened?"

The Purser licked his lips. He did not want to come out with the news. Then, with unintentional abruptness he announced, "I'm afraid Mr Portland's met with an accident, madam. One of the passengers found him in the swimming pool. The doctor seems to think it was a heart attack."

Stella's eyes glazed immediately. She looked round wildly as if searching. "Where is he? Where is Sam?"

"Well — ?"

Temple cut through the Purser's indecision. It was better to have the truth out and be done with the agony. "Is he dead?"

"Yes, sir."

The Purser's answer was almost a whisper but Stella heard it.

"Oh, no!" Her cry stopped all conversation in the bar. Every head turned towards the group by the window.

"Watch out, Paul! She's . . . "

Temple had forestalled Steve's warning. He had seen Stella sway and caught her as her eyes rolled upwards and her knees buckled.

The tragedy cast its shadow over the rest of the voyage, though deaths on board luxury liners were not uncommon. The average age of the passengers was high and it was not unknown for invalids to go on cruises merely for the sake of the excellent medical attention that was available. But the doctors had been unable to do anything for Sam Portland. He was dead before they hauled him out of the swimming pool and though the most modern techniques of resuscitation had been applied all was to no avail.

Temple had gone up to the Health Centre and in view of his reputation was allowed to see the body. He could find no reason to query the doctor's conviction that the portly American had suffered a heart attack. He had been unable to ascertain whether he had any previous history of heart trouble. Stella Portland was prostrate with shock and grief and she had been sedated by the doctor. Steve, who felt very close to the tragedy, had gone to the Portlands' suite next day to see if she could be of any comfort, but George Kelly had told her that Stella was either unable or unwilling to see anyone.

The Temples had tried to make the best they could of the remaining three days of the crossing. Steve had got her sea legs well enough to become a regular visitor to the shopping arcade where such firms as Harrods, Cartier, Turnbull and Asser, Gucci had displays. Temple spent some of his time in the well-stocked library and in the business centre and kept himself fit in between times in the health spa. The sea behaved itself until the very last night, when a storm blew up. Steve was glad when they sailed into the tranquil waters of the Solent on a predictably overcast October afternoon.

George Kelly had spoken to Portland's London office on the telephone and informed his representative there of the tragedy. Hubert Greene would be coming down to

Southampton to collect Mrs Portland by car. Rather
reluctantly Kelly had passed on Temple's request that
Portland's London representative should see him as soon as
he came aboard the ship.

They met by arrangement in the library, which was
disused, apart from the librarian, who was checking
returned books. Temple whiled away the time of waiting by
reading *Stalker*.

"Mr Temple?"

Greene had come into the library through the door
behind him.

Temple put his book down and stood up to face him.

"Yes."

"I'm Hubert Greene. I understand you want to see me?"

Hubert Greene was obviously a man of strong personality.
He wanted to dispel any possible impression that he was at
Temple's beck and call. His tone was faintly challenging. He
was tall, even taller than Temple, and wore his clothes well.

"Yes. Do sit down, Mr Greene."

Greene chose a leather-upholstered, fairly upright arm
chair. He crossed his legs, tweaked one trouser-leg and
checked the alignment of his cuffs.

"This is a most distressing business. I've just been on the
'phone to Moira . . . "

"Have you seen Mrs Portland yet?"

"No. I came up here as requested by you."

"Moira's Portland's daughter?"

"Yes – by his first marriage of course. The poor girl is
heart-broken."

"I rather expected Miss Portland to come on board with
you."

"No, as a matter of fact she couldn't leave town so I . . ."
Greene checked and shot Temple a wary look. "Do you
know Moira?"

"No, but her father spoke to me about her. I understand
she works for you."

"Well, she's attached to my office, yes." The corners of
Greene's mouth turned down and he tilted his head wryly.
"Whether she does any work or not is open to question.
Poor Sam! He thought the world of Moira." Greene's
expression suddenly changed. He uncrossed his legs and
leant forward, quizzing Temple. "How did this business

21

happen? You know, it seems perfectly extraordinary to me. Do you think he did have a heart attack, Mr Temple or . . . "

"Or what?"

"Or was it an accident?"

"The doctor seems convinced it was a heart attack," Temple answered him blandly.

Greene stared at him for a second before shooting his next question.

"How well did you know Sam?"

"Not very well, I'm afraid. We met for the first – and the last time unfortunately – on Friday morning."

"Sam was a great guy," Greene said with warm enthusiasm "A real American. That's the only way you can describe him."

"Was he an American?"

"But of course!" Greene exclaimed, surprised by the question.

"I mean, was he born in America?"

"Why yes, I've always thought so. I was always under the impression he was born in Chicago."

"I think perhaps I ought to tell you, Greene, before we go any further," Temple spoke slowly, emphasising his words, "Portland took me into his confidence. He told me why he was coming to England."

Greene took that on board thoughtfully. "He did?"

"Yes."

"Well, I hope you won't say anything about it, Temple. Now that the old boy's dead, I don't see any reason why we should go ahead. After all, it puts rather a different complexion on it. Don't you agree?"

"Yes, but if you've no objection, I'd like you to do me a favour."

"By all means. What is it?"

"I want you to introduce me to Mr Madison."

"Mr Madison?" Greene repeated the name as if it meant nothing to him.

"Yes," said Temple, watching him.

"Who's Mr Madison?"

"Why, he's the private inquiry agent, the man you . . ." Temple broke off. In a few seconds this affair had taken a whole new twist. "Are you trying to tell me that you've never heard of Madison?"

"Of course I haven't heard of him," Greene said with exasperation. "Who is he?"

"Two weeks ago you telexed Portland with the news that a private detective called Madison had discovered information concerning his identity."

Greene shook his head, more bewildered than ever. "Whose identity? Portland's?"

"Yes."

"Look here, I don't want to be rude, Temple, but have you been drinking?"

"You've never heard of Madison?"

Greene met Temple's level gaze steadily. "I've already told you that I haven't."

"Then why was Sam Portland in such a hurry to get to England?"

Greene reached into his pocket and brought out a packet of cigarettes. The librarian, standing on his library steps above and behind him, gave a loud cough. The library was a 'No Smoking' area. Greene put his cigarettes away again. "I thought you knew why. You said he told you. I was having trouble with Moira. I've been having trouble with her for weeks now. The girl's a little bi– well she gets completely out of hand. I tried to keep it from Sam but in the end it was quite impossible. Three days ago I made up my mind that I wasn't going to stand any more of her damned nonsense. I telexed her father and offered my resignation."

"I see."

"If you don't believe me, ask George Kelly." Greene had already stood up. "He knows about Moira, he knows what's been going on. Now, if you'll excuse me, I've got to see if Mrs Portland is ready to be taken down to the car."

Temple did not stand up. He responded in kind to Greene's curt nod. His head did not turn as the other man walked past him and out through the door behind. He sat there quite still for several minutes before he stood up and followed Portland's London representative.

"Paul, I do wish you'd get out of my way."

"Now don't be irritable, Steve!"

"Darling, we've been away for two weeks and I'm trying to unpack!"

The Temples were back at their flat in Eaton Square by

seven o'clock. Charlie had prepared a special welcome-home dinner, which the Temples had felt bound to savour to the full. Then there had been the inevitable pile of correspondence which Temple had sifted through to find out if there was anything of immediate importance. In the end it was ten o'clock before they even started to unpack their suitcases and the extra packages of duty-free goods they had bought on board ship.

"Yes, all right! All right, Steve! Where's that bow tie – the one I bought in New York?"

"Now what on earth do you want that for?"

"I want to try it on."

"You can't try it on now, not in your pyjamas, you'll look ridiculous. Besides, you've been trying it on ever since you bought it!"

"Oh, here it is!" Temple deftly tied the bow and studied the effect in the mirror. His expression changed from enthusiasm to gloom.

"I think it's a bit bright."

"Of course it's too bright, I told you that in the shop."

"It looked all right in New York."

"Yes, well, we're not in New York! Paul, go into your study and read a book or get into bed or have a bath or something!"

"By Timothy, I am popular!"

"You're just getting in my way, darling! Now where did I put that blouse? Oh, here it is . . . Come in, Charlie!"

Charlie was the Temples' Jack-of-all-trades — cook, housemaid, watch-dog and even driver, but the latter only in time of dire necessity. He stood five-foot six in his socks, which were all he had on his feet now. Above them he was wearing a pair of overtight chef's trousers and an old cardigan that had been buttoned up skew-whiff. He stared goggle-eyed at his master in pyjama top and dazzling bow tie.

"What is it, Charlie?"

"Sir Graham Forbes is here, sir. He'd like to have a word with you."

"Sir Graham? I didn't hear the door-bell."

"No, sir. You and Mrs Temple was kickin' up quite a racket. I put him in the living room, was that all right, sir?"

"Yes, that's all right, Charlie."

Still mesmerised by the tie, Charlie withdrew. Steve exchanged a worried glance with her husband.

"Paul, what does he want – do you know?"

"No, darling. Where's my dressing-gown?"

"It's on the bed."

"Oh, thanks . . . "

Temple put on his dressing-gown and thrust his feet into slippers. Steve's voice stopped him when he was at the door.

"Paul."

"Yes?"

"I shouldn't wear the tie, darling."

Sir Graham Forbes was the kind of man who seemed to fill any room he was in. Broad shoulders, a trim moustache and bushy eyebrows enhanced his commanding features. He was old enough to treat women with an avuncular protectiveness to which they reacted favourably. Steve always flirted with him shamelessly, knowing that he would never overstep the bounds of correctness.

"Hello, Steve!" he greeted her, as she came into the sitting-room a minute or two after Paul. The two men already had glasses of whisky in their hands. "My word, you do look well!" His eyes ran appreciatively over the silk house-robe she had put on. "Are you glad to be home?"

"Well, I don't know, Sir Graham. It all depends what you've got up your sleeve!"

"I haven't got anything up my sleeve," Forbes protested, a little too emphatically. "So don't worry, my dear!"

"Well, Sir Graham, is this a social call?" Temple asked, waving his guest to a chair.

"Not exactly. I want some information." Forbes sipped his whisky appreciatively and put the glass down on a low table beside his chair. "When you were on the boat coming over from America did you meet a man called Portland – Sam Portland?"

Temple nodded. "Yes, we did."

"Did you see much of him?"

"Well – I had quite a chat with him. As a matter of fact I was going to 'phone you. There's something about Portland you ought to know."

Steve was standing behind the sofa. "Don't you think you ought to start the story at the beginning, darling?" she suggested.

"Well," Temple began, "we left America last Friday evening. I was feeling rather tired because I'd had a pretty hectic time. It was just after six o'clock when the boat sailed. Steve was on deck staring at the skyscrapers and waving a last farewell to New York . . . "

Sir Graham listened without interruption while Temple told him in detail what had occurred on the *Princess Diana*. He ended with an account of his conversation with Hubert Greene.

"Did you speak to George Kelly?"

"Yes. He confirmed Greene's story. He said he'd actually seen the telex from Hubert Greene offering Portland his resignation."

"Did you ask him about Madison?"

"He'd never heard of him."

"M'm." Forbes sounded sceptical about that. He picked up his glass and tipped his head back to empty it. Temple stood up to replenish both their glasses.

"Sir Graham, how does Scotland Yard come into this?"

"Just over a week ago one of my men – Chief Inspector James – received this note. Here we are, Steve, read it."

Steve had seated herself on the end of the sofa. She reached over for the note and slowly read it out. " 'An American multi-millionaire called Sam Portland intends to visit England. He must be stopped from doing so – if he isn't . . . a . . . murder . . . will . . . be . . . committed.' "

"Is there a signature?" Temple asked.

"No, it's typed, darling. There's no signature."

"At first we thought it was a hoax," Forbes said, recovering the note from Steve. "Then something came up which made James decide to take it seriously. He contacted New York. They checked up and told him that Portland apparently hadn't the slightest intention of coming to England."

"He probably hadn't at that time."

"We kept the file open but took no further action until we heard that Portland was on his way over here . . . "

". . . and had died of a heart attack," Temple finished for him.

"Precisely. Naturally we obtained a list of passengers and when I saw your name on it I was confident you could fill us in. There will have to be an inquest, of course, even though the doctor appeared quite happy to sign a death certificate attributing the cause of death as . . . " Forbes paused as there came a knock on the door and Charlie poked his head in.

"Excuse me, sir."

"What is it, Charlie?" Temple asked with ill-concealed impatience.

"There's a Mr Greene to see you, sir. I didn't say you was in."

"Surely it's a bit late for a social call," Steve protested.

"That's all right, Charlie," Temple said with resignation. "I'll see him."

Steve stood up and adjusted her house-robe more carefully. "What can Greene want, Paul?"

"We'll soon see," Temple murmured. He just had time to put the whisky glasses away before Charlie showed the visitor in. "Hello, Greene! Come in! What can I do for you?"

Greene was taken aback to find his hosts in night attire. "I'm awfully sorry to disturb you, especially at this time of night, but . . ." He was staring at Sir Graham, who had remained seated. "I beg your pardon, sir, but haven't we met before?"

"My name is Forbes," Sir Graham told him bluntly, as if that precluded any previous acquaintance.

"This is Sir Graham Forbes of Scotland Yard," Temple explained tactfully.

"Oh, I beg your pardon! I was under the impression that we'd met somewhere. How do you do, sir?" Greene was ready to follow up the introduction with a handshake but Sir Graham made no move to respond in kind, contenting himself with a nod.

"I think you've met my wife."

"Yes, we met at Southampton." Having been rebuffed once Greene did not offer to shake hands with Steve. "Good evening, Mrs Temple. Temple, I've just left Mrs Portland. She's in a pretty bad way, I'm afraid, and she seems very upset about — well — what seems to me rather a trivial matter."

"What is Mrs Portland upset about?"

"Well, it seems that somebody's stolen Mr Portland's watch-chain."

"Stolen his watch-chain?" It was Sir Graham that spoke.

"Yes."

"Was it very valuable?"

"From the way Stella's going on about it I should say extremely valuable."

Steve guessed that Mrs Portland had recovered from her shock sufficiently to give her late husband's London representative a very difficult time.

"She's probably thinking of the sentimental value."

"I daresay she is, Mrs Temple, but surely at a time like this . . . to bother about a watch-chain . . . it seems most odd."

"Have you been in touch with the shipping line?" Temple asked.

Greene was turning his head this way and that as questions came from three different directions.

"Yes, I've even been on to Southampton!"

Temple had deliberately not offered Greene a drink nor invited him to sit down. He had not forgotten the abrupt way the man had ended their conversation on *Princess Diana*.

"Well, quite frankly, I don't see what I can do."

"I was wondering if by any chance you can recall seeing the chain. If I remember rightly you saw Sam shortly after – after he died."

"The only time I saw it was the morning he introduced himself to me. It was a thin gold chain with an English penny on the end. He kept the penny in his waistcoat pocket."

"I don't know anything about that. All I know is I wish to goodness we could find the chain!"

"Where is Mrs Portland staying?"

"She's at the Ritz but there's some talk of her coming down to my place for the weekend."

"Is she alone?" Steve asked with some concern.

"No, George Kelly's with her and Moira's moving in tomorrow morning."

"Who's Moira?" Forbes wanted to know.

"It's her step-daughter."

"Have they met before, by the way?" Temple asked.

"Yes, they met about six months ago in New York."

As no one else had made a move to sit down Forbes abandoned his chair and got to his feet.

"Mr Greene, I understand from what Temple tells me,

that you're in charge of the Portland Corporation in this country."

"Yes, Sir Graham."

"When did you last see Portland?"

"About four years ago."

"Was Portland over here?"

"No, I was in America. So far as I know this was Sam's first trip to Europe." Greene had got the message that his intrusion so late in the evening had not made him exactly popular. He began to move towards the door. "Well, I'm sorry to have bothered you, Mr Temple. I thought perhaps you might be able to throw some light on the missing watch-chain."

"If I were you I should try and get in touch with the Purser."

"Yes, I'll do that."

"Can I give you a lift?" Forbes offered surprisingly. "I was just about to make a move."

"Well, actually I'm on my way to Park Lane. If you could drop me I'd be very grateful."

"Yes, certainly."

"Paul . . ." Steve had waited till she heard two doors closing, the front door and that of Charlie's own private little flatlet. "Do you think the doctor was mistaken about Portland? Do you think we've all been mistaken and – he was murdered?"

"No, I don't. But there's one thing I'm rather curious about, Steve."

"What's that – the watch-chain?"

"Yes. I'm going to have a word with Mrs Portland."

"Oh, darling, not at this time of night!"

Temple was already at the telephone table. "I've got a hunch it's important." He opened the telephone book and ran his finger down the column till he found the number.

Shaking her head half in exasperation and half in affection, Steve went to the drinks cabinet and poured herself a small measure of brandy. Behind her she heard Paul stabbing the numbers, talking to The Ritz switchboard and finally getting through to Mrs Portland's suite. Her voice came over loudly on the 'phone and Steve was able to hear both sides of the conversation.

"Mrs Portland? This is Paul Temple here."

"Oh, good evening, Mr Temple!"

Temple quickly distanced the 'phone a few inches from his ear. "Forgive me ringing at this time of the night, Mrs Portland, but I've just been having a chat with Mr Greene. He tells me that you've lost your husband's watch-chain."

"Is Hubert with you at the moment?"

"No, he's just this second left."

"I've got the chain, Mr Temple, there's no need to worry about it."

"You mean you've found it?"

"No, I mean it was never lost. I – I had it all the time."

"I see," said Temple, trying to conceal his annoyance at the false alarm.

"I doubt very much whether you do see, Mr Temple." Mrs Portland paused. "Are you likely to be passing my hotel tomorrow?"

"Yes, I might be. Probably in the morning."

"I'd like you to drop in for a few moments."

"Yes, all right. Shall we say eleven o'clock?"

"That will do nicely. Good-night, Mr Temple."

"Good night, Mrs Portland." Thoughtfully Temple put the receiver down. "You heard all that?"

"I couldn't help it, Paul. Why did Greene lie to you about it?"

"I don't think he was lying, darling. He really did think it was lost."

The Temples' flat was fitted with Banham double mortice locks on the front door and the latest burglar-proof double-glass windows. But Steve always insisted on having a window slightly open in the bedroom. She could not sleep unless she knew that there was an inlet for fresh air, even on the chilliest nights.

She had been the first to put her light out and soon afterwards Temple had closed his book and followed suit. But his sleep was not deep. In his subconscious mind he kept running over the short conversations he had had with Forbes and Greene and checking back on his encounter with Sam Portland. He heard the gentle chimes of the clock in the sitting-room striking two and soon after that he must have dropped off completely.

Perhaps an hour later he woke up. The only sound was

the muted hum of the radio-alarm on his bedside table and the echo of a car in the square below. He tried to recall the faint noise that had alerted him, more like a furtive creak than a sharp crack. He felt a stronger current of air on his face and the rustle of the curtains stirring at the window. Opening his eyes he saw pale moonlight slanting across the balcony outside. Was the chink in the curtains wider than when he had gone to bed?

Then for a moment the shaft of moonlight was broken as a shadow passed across.

Very quietly Temple pushed the covers back and swung his legs out of the bed. His movement woke Steve.

"Paul . . . "

"Sh," he whispered. "There's someone on the balcony. Don't talk."

She froze. He could sense her fear as she held her breath. There was no further movement at the window. Temple sat completely motionless for five minutes. Through the wall he could just hear a faint sound like waves on a pebbly beach. It was Charlie, snoring in his sleep.

At last that creak came again. The curtains swung slightly. Again the moonlight was broken by a shadow. Someone had come through the window and was standing behind the curtains. Temple still made no movement except to put a reassuring hand on Steve's arm. All his antennae were on full alert. He sensed rather than saw the intruder move out from behind the heavy curtain, into the pool of darkness in the corner beside the door. He could smell the faint tang that always clings to clothes of a heavy smoker.

Reaching towards the bed-head he pulled the string to switch on his reading lamp. Sudden light flooded the room.

The man who already had his hand on the door-handle whipped round, blinking and momentarily dazzled. He was tall, fiercely moustachioed, heavily built, fortyish and scared. In his hand he gripped a stubby automatic.

Temple said, in his normal conversational tone, "Are you looking for anything in particular, my friend – or is this just a social call?"

"Stay where you are! Don't move either of you!"

Temple had faced men with guns before and he already had the measure of this one. By the way he was holding his weapon he was no trained marksman. But he was scared and that was always the danger.

Temple did not obey the command. He shuffled his feet into the slippers he had discarded before going to bed, stood up and put on his dressing-gown.

"Paul, he's got a gun!"

"Yes, darling. I can see it."

"Now don't try anything!" the man warned. "I'm prepared to use it."

"I'm sure you are," said Temple. "Just tell me what you're looking for and I'll try to help you."

"You can help me by putting your hands up and standing against that wall. No, facing it. And keep your hands up!"

"Paul, for God's sake do as he says!"

Temple did as he was told, feigning submission. He heard the man padding across the room behind him, suspicious that he had some weapon in the pocket of his dressing-gown. This was almost too good to be true. The man was obviously a novice. He smelt the whisky on his breath as he came close. The nose of the automatic was pressed hard against the small of his back. A hand groped in the pocket of his dressing-gown.

At that critical moment and in a lightning movement Temple's arm flailed down like the blade of a propeller. The side of his stiffened hand connected brutally with the man's wrist, knocking his hand sideways and loosening his grip. The automatic clattered to the floor. Temple's movement had swung his body round to face his assailant.

Paradoxically he was more dangerous now. Deprived of his gun he had to rely on weapons with which he was more familiar – his fists.

Temple, himself no mean boxer, had aimed an uppercut at his jaw. The man parried it expertly, then jabbed Temple viciously low in the stomach. The blow doubled him up gasping for breath and he felt the side of an open hand smash down on his neck behind the ear.

He saw a white flash and slumped to the ground.

"I thought you were never coming, Paul! I've poured your coffee out."

"Oh, thanks, darling."

"I've told Charlie to make you an om[...]
right?"

"Yes, that's fine."

"How does your head feel this morning?"

"It's not too bad. I could kick myself for letting [...]
get away!"

"Do you know, Paul," she said now, remembering [...]
behaviour with shame, "although I was worried I ha[...]
most terrible fit of the giggles. I just couldn't help myself."

"I don't know why the devil you didn't hit him with
something! I'm afraid you didn't come up to scratch,
darling!"

"You didn't exactly come up to scratch yourself!" Steve
flashed back. Then she relented and put a hand on her
injured husband's arm. "Have you been in touch with the
Yard?"

"Yes, I spoke to Superintendent Vosper. He's calling
round after breakfast." Paul cocked his ear at the sound of
the front door bell. "Perhaps that's him now."

A minute later Charlie appeared at the door of the dining-
room. He looked haggard after his broken night's sleep. "I
beg your pardon, Mrs T."

"Yes, what is it, Charlie?"

"There's a Mrs Portland's called – she wants to see Mr
Temple."

Steve turned to Temple in surprise. "I thought you'd
arranged to see Mrs Portland at her hotel?"

"I did. I said I'd drop in about eleven." Temple shrugged.
"It's all right, Charlie, you can show her in."

Steve would hardly have recognised the woman who
walked in as the Stella Portland she had met on her second
evening on board ship. She was wearing a dark grey
costume, the nearest thing to black that she possessed, and
had aged by ten years. Gone was her confident, contented
manner. She clearly felt it was no longer worth while taking
trouble over her make-up and her eyes were red from
weeping.

Steve rose to meet the American, her face showing
concern.

"Good morning, Mrs Portland. We're just having some
coffee, won't you join us?"

[...] rs Temple." Stella's voice was [...] 'A cup of coffee certainly

[...] ulling a chair back for her. [...] very well last night." Stella [...] self together. She gave a [...] ust been for a walk in St [...] t it? You know, there's no [...] know why, but I always [...] would have loved it over [...] . . . " The brief attempt at [...] had failed. She closed her eyes and [...] back a sob.

"Do sit down, Mrs Portland."

Stella took the proffered chair, as Charlie came in with another cup and saucer. No one spoke as Steve poured the coffee and pushed the milk and sugar towards her.

Then Temple remarked pleasantly, "I think we had an appointment at eleven o'clock."

"Yes, we did, Mr Temple." Stella was immediately contrite. "I'm awfully sorry dropping in on you like this."

"That's all right," Steve reassured her. "We're delighted to see you."

"I thought we might be able to talk better here than at my hotel, You see . . . " A hint of desperation crept into Stella's voice. "Mr Temple, did Sam talk to you about his watch-chain? Did he show it to you?"

"Yes, as a matter of fact he did. Mrs Portland, what is this all about?" Temple's voice also betrayed him, showed his impatience. "Hubert Greene came here last night, he told me that you'd lost the chain and yet when I telephoned you at your hotel you . . . "

"No, no, I haven't lost it. It's here. I want you to have a look at it, Mr Temple. Please . . . " Stella had opened her handbag. She produced a chain with a watch at one end and a shiny penny on the other. She handed it to Temple. "Is that the chain that my husband showed you?"

"Yes."

"Are you sure?"

Yes, I'm reasonably sure. It's got the penny on the end and it looks exactly the same. Yes, this is it all right."

"Did my husband tell you about the penny?"

"He said it was in his pocket when a policeman called Dan Kelly arrested him for jay walking. That was in Chicago in 1952."

"That's right," Stella confirmed.

"Your husband told me rather a remarkable story, Mrs Portland. He said that, from the moment he was arrested his memory was a complete blank and he simply couldn't recall . . . " Temple, turning the penny over in his hand, had stopped dead and was staring at it.

"Paul, what's the matter?"

Temple pushed the penny across the table. "Steve, look at the head on this penny!"

Steve examined the penny and looked at Paul, puzzled. "What about it?"

"That's Queen Elizabeth. She had not come to the throne when Portland was picked up in Chicago. Look at the date on the back."

Steve turned the penny over and shook her head in bewilderment. "1957!"

2 The Manila

"But that's impossible!" Stella exclaimed. "If the penny wasn't made until 1957 Sam couldn't have had it in his pocket when he was arrested."

"Exactly, Mrs Portland. When I met your husband, the first morning we left New York, he told me that although he was known as Sam Portland, Portland was not his real name. He told me that he didn't know his name, had no idea of his identity."

"That's perfectly true." Stella had added milk and sugar to her coffee. Now she began to stir it. "Thirty-five years ago a policeman called Dan Kelly found Sam wandering aimlessly down Portland Avenue in Chicago. He couldn't even remember who he was or where he'd come from. Is that the story my husband told you?"

"Part of it, yes. But he also told me that Hubert Greene, his London representative, had telexed him about a private detective called Madison."

"Madison?"

"Yes. He was supposed to have discovered something about your husband's past. When I spoke to Greene about this, he said it was nonsense, he'd never heard of Madison."

"I've never heard of him either! All this is news to me."

"Your husband went so far as to say that Madison was his sole reason for coming over here."

"But that's ridiculous! We all know why Sam wanted to come to England. Moira – his daughter – works over here and the silly girl's been making a fool of herself. She's got engaged to a smooth young man called Chris Boyer who spends most of his time in night clubs. He's forever taking Moira off to some place called the Manila. I know for a fact that Sam was very worried about it."

Stella lifted her cup and Steve thought that at last she was going to take a sip.

"Mrs Portland, you still haven't told us about the watch-chain."

36

"Oh yes, I was forgetting." Stella put the cup down again. "Just before we left New York, Sam said rather a peculiar thing, as a matter of fact I thought he was joking. He said, 'If anything should happen to me, Stella, take great care of my watch-chain. You'll probably find it's the most valuable thing I possess.'"

"He didn't mention the penny at all?"

"No," said Stella, at last putting the cup to her lips.

"Mrs Portland," Steve asked, "why did you tell Hubert Greene that the chain was missing?"

"Because he was so curious about it. All the way back from Southampton he kept on about the chain, throwing out veiled hints that he'd like to see it." Stella pursed her lips. "I made up my mind I wasn't going to let him see it."

"Well, it looks a perfectly ordinary watch-chain." Temple had continued to examine it carefully. "The only curious point is the date on the penny."

"Yes, that worries me. It almost makes me think that Sam wasn't telling the truth, that the story about himself was a fabrication."

"Well, that's one explanation, of course, but there is another, a very simple one. Somebody's changed the penny."

The inquest on Sam Portland was held five days later at Southampton. Temple had been unable to attend as he was already committed to delivering a lecture that morning on the implications of genetic fingerprinting. Sir Graham Forbes had implied that he would be going down and had promised to call in that evening.

Temple was in his study working on the first chapter of his new book when he heard the door-bell ring. He glanced at the wall-clock. It was only three-forty-five. Half a minute later he heard Forbes' strong and clear accents in the hall. He pushed his chair back and went to the door.

"Hello, Sir Graham. I didn't expect you back so soon. Did you go to the inquest?"

"No, I'm absolutely up to my eyes. I sent Raine. He 'phoned half an hour ago. I tried to call you but only got the ansaphone."

"Come on in and tell me what happened. I'm afraid I was working on my new book."

Forbes accepted the invitation and sat down on the button-upholstered armchair.

"For your information Mr Samuel L. Portland died from natural causes. The Coroner was quite convinced there was no suspicion of foul play."

Temple had pressed the stop switch on his ansaphone and resumed his seat behind the desk. "Well, if the Coroner was convinced . . . "

"Don't you agree?"

"There's something behind this Portland business. I don't know what but I'm quite sure there is."

"Now, take the facts, Temple." Forbes sounded a little impatient. "Either Portland told you the truth about himself and about Hubert Greene getting in touch with him – in which case Greene lied to you when you saw him at Southampton – or Portland didn't tell you the truth, in which case his story was a complete hoax."

"There are too many coincidences for my liking," Temple persisted. "First of all you receive an anonymous letter saying that if Portland comes over here a murder will be committed . . . "

"But a murder hasn't been committed."

"One very nearly was committed, Sir Graham," Temple pointed out quietly.

"When?"

"Five nights ago, here, in this very flat."

"Yes," Forbes conceded, "But we've no evidence that had any connection with the Portland case."

Temple decided not to press the point. "Anyway, let's forget it for the time being. Would you like a cup of tea, Sir Graham?"

"No thanks. I suppose I'd better be getting back to the Yard. Heaven knows there's enough to do."

"What are you on at the moment?"

"What are we not on? Bomb scares, the state visit, a spate of armed robberies. We're particularly worried about this counterfeit business. I expect you've read about it?"

"No, but I've been abroad for two weeks."

"It's serious, Temple. For several months now the Continent has been flooded with counterfeit notes – chiefly dollars, of course. About a week ago the French Sûreté said that in their opinion the gang were not actually working from the Continent but from England."

"Who are the people behind it – have you any idea?"

"I wouldn't say this to anyone else, Temple, but frankly, at the moment we haven't a clue. So now you know why I'm not particularly interested in the late Mr Portland, to say nothing of the watch-chain."

The telephone on the desk had been ringing for several seconds. "Excuse me." Temple said and picked the receiver up. "Hello?"

"Paul, I've been trying to ring you but all I got was the ansaphone."

"I'm sorry, Steve. Where are you?"

"Paul, listen." Steve's voice was excited. "I'm in Harridge's. I want you to come here straight away. It's urgent."

"What's happened?"

Forbes had made a valedictory sign to Temple and was moving towards the hall. Temple signalled him to wait.

"I came back from Bramley on the 11.40. When I got to Waterloo I was just getting into a taxi when . . . Paul, are you listening?"

"Yes of course I'm listening. You were just getting into a taxi."

"Yes, and I saw a man join the end of the taxi queue. At first I couldn't place him. Then suddenly I realised who it was. Darling, it was *that* man."

"Which man?"

"The man who broke into the flat, the man who knocked you out."

Forbes had come back into the room and was trying to hear what the caller was saying.

"Are you sure?"

"Absolutely sure."

"Go on, Steve . . . "

"I didn't know what to do. I made my driver wait a bit and then when I saw him getting into a taxi I decided to follow him. He's here at Harridge's."

"Where are you actually speaking from?"

"I'm in a 'phone booth on the ground floor, you know, next to the flower stall."

"Where's the man?"

"He's in the snack-bar. It's all right, he can't come out

without my seeing him, in any case he's only just given his order."

"Has he seen you?"

"No, I don't think so."

"O.K., darling. Now, don't do anything foolish. I'll be there in ten minutes." Temple slammed the receiver down and stood up.

"What's happened?"

"Get your hat, Sir Graham. I'll explain in the car."

The lift was occupied. Rather than wait for it Temple raced down the stairs, with Forbes not far behind. His Jaguar was parked almost directly opposite the flat. He was in the driving seat and had the engine started before Forbes slid in beside him. The car had pulled out from the kerb before Sir Graham had time to fasten his seat-belt.

"You'll cover me if I get stopped for speeding, Sir Graham?"

"What's this—" Forbes was still regaining his breath. "What's this all about?"

As soon as he heard that Steve had spotted the burglar at Harridge's Forbes used the in-car telephone to contact his office at Scotland Yard. Temple concentrated on his driving. The knowledge that Steve was perfectly capable of attempting to prevent her quarry from leaving made him take chances. Forbes closed his eyes as Temple raced across the King's Road just as the lights went red. Through Belgrave Square the tyres were shrieking. Down the narrows of Pont Street he switched on his headlamps and used his horn ruthlessly to clear a passage. As he swung right into Sloane Street the car heeled over and Forbes was only prevented from falling into his lap by the seat-belt.

Traffic was already building up to the evening rush hour and it was seven minutes before the tall Harridge's building came in sight. There was no hope of finding a parking space anywhere near the store. Temple double-parked close to the entrance which he knew was nearest the flower stall. He left Forbes to deal with a scandalised traffic warden who was gesticulating wildly.

He spotted Steve as soon as he burst through the swing doors. She was standing beside the flower stall at the top of the steps that led down into the snack-bar. She was pale with tension.

"Thank goodness, Paul! You've been quick."

"Is he still here?"

"Yes. At that table over by the window. He's just paying his bill."

Using a floral display for cover Temple peered into the snack-bar. The man's face was in profile. He had no doubt it was the intruder of five nights ago.

Forbes had come in hot on Temple's heels.

"Hello, Steve. He's still here?"

"Yes, Sir Graham."

"Vosper's outside. He's putting men on all the exits. We'll soon have this place sealed up."

"It's our man all right," Temple said, moving back out of sight.

"Steve, is this the only exit from the snack-bar?"

"Yes, I think – watch out, Paul! He's coming this way!"

The man had risen from his seat clutching a Samsonite suitcase. He started towards the steps at the top of which Steve and the two men were waiting. Whether he spotted Steve or was warned by some instinct no one would ever know. He halted abruptly, then turned on his heel and ran towards the door which led to the kitchen. A waitress entering with a loaded tray was bowled over by the heavy suitcase.

"Stay here, Steve," Temple commanded, as he raced down the flight of stairs and through the tables of the snack-bar.

He had to step across the fallen waitress and the scattered dishes to push open the door leading to the kitchen. The chefs in their white coats and cylindrical hats had stopped work and were gaping at the wild figure which was already at the tradesman's entrance, struggling with one hand to open the door.

Temple gained ground on his quarry through the kitchen. Outside on the pavement he had to pause for a moment. Which way had the man with the suitcase gone? Then he saw him, twenty yards away, heading for the busy High Street. For someone burdened with a heavy suitcase he was moving fast. Temple gained on him again during the short sprint to the main thoroughfare. The entrance to an Underground station yawned invitingly beyond the stream of traffic. The man threw one backward glance over his shoulder, then made his fatal mistake. Missing the warning painted on the roadway to LOOK LEFT, he looked right and walked straight into the path of a taxi bowling fast along the bus lane against the stream of traffic.

The taxi driver slammed on his brakes but it was too late. The man was caught by the front mudguard and slammed against a lamp standard. Temple heard the sickening crunch of his head against the solid metal. The suitcase was projected fifteen feet along the gutter.

"Sorry we've been so long, Steve."

Half an hour had passed before Temple and Forbes were able to rejoin Steve in the snack-bar. They found her starting on her third cup of coffee.

"What happened?"

"He was killed, Steve," Forbes told her. "Went straight under a taxi. It must have been instantaneous."

"Oh Paul, I feel awful." Steve shook her head, near to tears.

"Now Steve, listen, there's no point in reproaching yourself about this," Forbes reassured her. "If he hadn't run for it this wouldn't have happened."

"No, I suppose not. Who was he, do you know?"

"According to this diary which we found on him, his name's Mark Kendell." Forbes had the diary open at the first page. "78A Nelson Towers, Chelsea. I'll get Vosper to check that."

"Anything else of interest?" Temple had sat down beside Steve and put a hand on her arm to comfort her.

"No, there doesn't seem to be. Just a minute." Forbes was flicking through the pages of the diary. "Apparently he had a date this evening. October 19th 8.45. The Manila. Appointment with C.B."

"The Manila?" Temple echoed. "That name's familiar."

"Yes, don't you remember, darling? Mrs Portland mentioned it. She said that her step-daughter was engaged . . . Now that's funny. She said that her step-daughter was engaged to a man called Chris Boyer, who regularly frequents the Manila Club."

"C.B.," said Temple. "Don't you think there are too many coincidences here, Sir Graham?"

"M-m," Forbes conceded. "It looks as if Kendell really was mixed up in the Portland affair."

"And he broke into our flat thinking we had the watch-chain?" Temple saw, not without alarm, that his wife's face had an expression which he knew all too well. It meant she was hot on the scent of something.

"Paul, wouldn't it be an idea if we went along to the Manila Club tonight and simply asked Boyer if he had an appointment with this man Mark Kendell?"

"Quite an idea," Temple said without enthusiasm, "but unfortunately neither of us happens to be a member of the Manila."

To his exasperation, Forbes said with a grin, "We can easily get over that, Temple."

"Don't say you're a member, Sir Graham," said Steve.

"No, but Archie Brooks is. He'll fix you up all right."

"Who's Archie Brooks?"

"One of our best undercover men. We keep him on tap for occasions like this. I'll tell him to meet you both at the Manila at ten o'clock. Is that all right?"

"Fine," said Temple with a resigned shrug.

"Well, I'll get back to the Yard." Forbes was turning away when a uniformed constable came into the snack-bar. He was carrying the Samsonite suitcase. "We found the key to this in the deceased's pocket, sir," he told Forbes. "The Inspector said he'd prefer you to open it."

The PC handed the suitcase over. Forbes was taken unawares by the weight. It dragged his arm and shoulder down.

"I say, it's pretty heavy, isn't it? I wonder what the fellow was carrying in it."

Forbes heaved the case up onto the table. Temple, Steve and the PC crowded behind him as he inserted the key in the lock. It opened with a snap. Forbes released the two side catches and lifted the lid.

"By Timothy!" Temple whispered.

Inside, tightly packed, were row upon row of neat bundles of notes. Forbes picked one of the packets up, stared at the top note for a moment then silently handed the bundle to Temple.

Temple took it and whistled.

"What are they, Paul?"

"Hundred dollar bills, Steve. Brand new ones. There's a small fortune here."

The Manila Club was at the western end of the King's Road, Chelsea. The entrance was unostentatious. The heavy panelled door had once been that of a private town house. It was permanently closed and only opened when arrivals identified themselves on the entry 'phone.

"Mr and Mrs Paul Temple."

"Are you a member, sir?"

"No, but I'm meeting Mr Brooks."

The door buzzed and swung open. At once the muffled thud of amplified dance music became audible. The sound was to be a background to every conversation in the club, even drowning the babel of voices from the crowded rooms. A dark muscular man in a purple velvet jacket was coming down the passage to meet them as the door clicked shut again.

"Mr Brooks is expecting you, sir. He's in the cocktail bar. You can leave your coats here."

There was a hatch half way down the passage, where a pretty girl wearing a tambourine-shaped hat exchanged numbered tickets for their coats. Temple folded both tickets and put them in his waistcoat pocket.

"I'll be with you in a moment, Paul." Steve had seen the sign indicating the ladies' powder room. It depicted a Spanish senorita in a swirling flamenco skirt.

Left to kick his heels Temple was staring over the heads of the crowd in the cocktail bar when he heard a familiar voice behind him at the cloakroom hatch.

"My hat and coat, please," it said in peremptory tones.

"Have you got the ticket, sir?"

"I've got the thing somewhere," the man said, searching his pockets. "It was number 74 . . . Ah, here it is!"

Still unruffled the girl took the ticket and disappeared to fetch the coat and hat. Drumming impatiently on the counter with his fingers, the man half turned and Temple saw who it was.

"Oh, hello, Greene. I didn't expect to see you here."

Hubert Greene was equally surprised but he covered it quickly. "Oh, hello, Temple. What are you doing here?"

"Strange though it may seem, I sometimes frequent this type of establishment."

"You're welcome, it's not my idea of fun and games."

"No. What is your idea of fun and games?"

Greene gave Temple an amused look. "Reading Shakespeare and playing chess. Do you play chess, Mr Temple?"

"Indifferently, I'm afraid."

"Well," said Greene blandly, "that's my idea of fun and games."

The brief exchange had had the flavour of a verbal duelling match. The voice of the cloakroom girl cut cheerfully into it.

"Your hat and coat, sir."

"Oh, thank you."

Greene took the coat and hat but did not put them on. He seemed to be waiting for someone. His eyes searched the crowd behind Temple.

"Are you a member here?" Temple inquired.

"No, but Moira Portland is. I dropped in to have a word with her."

"Is she here tonight?"

"Yes, she's with her fiancé, Chris Boyer. The silly girl's here every night. I wish to goodness someone would talk to her, Temple."

Temple wondered if he was supposed to fulfil that role. "Oh, what about?"

"She doesn't seem to realise that now the old man's dead a great deal of responsibility's going to fall on her shoulders." Instead of making for the door Greene began to walk back towards the cocktail bar. Temple fell in beside him, still keeping an eye open for Steve.

"There's going to be a lot of work to do during the next three or four months. This is no time for fooling around. I am afraid this chap Boyer is a very bad influence on her."

"Is that what you've been telling her?"

"No, I've been trying to persuade her to come down to my place for the weekend. I've got Mrs Portland staying with me and the old boy's secretary, George Kelly. There's a great deal to discuss, Temple."

"Yes, I can well imagine it," Temple murmured. He was still wondering why Greene was confiding the family's problems to him.

"Moira refuses to come unless I invite Chris Boyer. Why the devil should I invite him?" Greene threw Temple an angry glance. "Quite apart from the fact that I can't abide the fellow, he's not a member of the family and he's got nothing whatever to do with the business."

"Well, it looks as if he's going to be a member of the family, doesn't it?"

"I wouldn't be too sure about that. This isn't the first boy friend Moira's lost her head over." Greene lowered his voice. "Hello, here they are."

Temple had no trouble in picking out the couple who had come up the stairs from the disco in the cellar. The girl was about twenty-six, with attractive features and a good figure. She was laughing excitedly as she looked up into the face of the man beside her. He was very tall, very dark, very slim, with Mediterranean good looks.

Moira's face became half amused, half defiant when she saw Greene.

"Hello, Hubert, I thought you'd gone."

"I'm just leaving, Moira. This is Mr Temple."

"Hello," said Moira, hardly glancing at Temple. "We're just going to have a drink, Hubert. Won't you join us?"

"No, thank you."

Moira laughed at him mockingly "You can have an orangeade, darling."

"I don't like orangeade," said Greene quietly.

"Oh, I quite forgot. It's ginger-ale, isn't it?" Moira smiled up at Boyer. Her little performance had been put on for his benefit.

"Goodbye, Mr—" She was looking at Temple directly for the first time. "Did you say your name was Temple?"

"Mr Greene said so – yes."

"I've heard Stella talk about you." Moira's manner was suddenly serious. "You know who I mean, don't you? Stella Portland, my step-mother."

"Yes, we met on the boat coming over from America."

"That must have been cosy," said Moira sarcastically "Oh, this is my fiancé Chris Boyer."

Boyer nodded his head respectfully. "Glad to know you, Mr Temple. This is quite an honour. I've heard a great deal about you."

"From Mrs Portland?"

"No, no. I mean I've read about you in the newspapers. I gather you're the best known private eye in Europe."

"Private eye isn't a description I care for," said Temple. "But I wonder if Mr Madison shares that opinion?"

"Mr Madison?"

"He's a private detective. You haven't heard of him?"

Boyer shook his head and turned to Moira for enlightenment, but the name had obviously meant nothing to her either.

"Come on, Chris." Moira grabbed her fiancé's arm. "You dance divinely but, boy, it does make a girl thirsty."

"Goodbye, Moira," Greene said, with a last attempt to be friendly. "I hope I shall see you at the weekend — both of you."

It was Boyer who had the grace to acknowledge the invitation. "That's nice of you. We shall be delighted, shan't we, Moira?"

But Moira was not listening. Greene turned to Temple with an exasperated expression, as if to say "You see what I'm up against!"

Temple had at last spotted Steve coming out of the powder room. As he watched her coming through the crowd towards him he thought how favourably she compared with Moira's somewhat exaggerated prettiness. Greene nodded to Steve, barely acknowledging her presence, then made his excuses and departed.

"Is he a member here?" Steve asked as she watched him go.

"No, he only dropped in to have a word with Moira. Now, I believe we'll find our man in the cocktail bar. I'll lead the way, you follow me."

There was such a crush that Temple had to literally force his way into the bar. A row of freakishly dressed young men were propping up the bar and obviously enjoying themselves.

"I wonder which of these characters is Archie Brooks?" Temple said over his shoulder.

"I'll bet a tenner that's him."

"Where?"

"Second from the left. He's an Archie if ever I saw one!"

"Well, you'll lose your tenner!" Steve's head jerked round at the voice from behind her. "I'm much better looking than that."

She was looking into a jovial, friendly and slightly chubby face.

"Mrs Temple?"

"Yes," Steve admitted, deeply embarrassed.

"I'm Archie Brooks." Her hand was seized in a strong, dry hand-clasp. "Is this your husband?"

"Yes."

"Glad to meet you, Temple. Heard an awful lot about you from Sir Graham. Odd we haven't met before."

"Yes, it is. I hope this date hasn't inconvenienced you?"

"Not in the slightest." Archie Brooks raised his voice to over-ride the din. "By the way, shall we go straight to our table? This place is a bit like a bear garden."

"Yes, I think it's a good idea," Steve said with relief.

"Can you push your way through the bods, Mrs Temple, or shall I shout fire?"

"I think I can manage." Steve began to push her way towards the door that led to the restaurant.

"Hello, Chunky." A young man with a military style moustache wearing an unsuitably loud check jacket had spotted Brooks and bull-dozed his way towards him. "How are you?"

"Hello, George." Brooks took it calmly. "How's things?"

"Ghastly!"

"Where's Edith?"

"She's in Tenby, old boy. Been there for six months."

"Tenby?"

"Yes."

"How very odd."

"It's all very difficult, Chunky. Tell you next time we meet."

George melted back into the crowd. Archie waited till they were clear of the cocktail bar before explaining. "That was George Denson."

"I gathered that." Steve was still smiling.

"We were at school together," Archie said, as if that explained everything.

"Why did he call you Chunky?"

"Everybody calls me Chunky, Mrs Temple." Archie laughed. "Do you know those tins of beautiful pineapple chunks – delicious?"

"Yes," Steve nodded. She could not help liking this ebullient character.

"Well, I used to eat thousands of 'em when I was at school. Simply couldn't stop. Tin after tin." Archie shook his head in wonderment at his own prowess. "By golly, I've eaten some pineapple chunks in my time."

The policy of the new owners of the Manila had been to broaden the appeal of the club and to encourage members to dine there instead of coming along later in the evening after eating in a restaurant. Acquisition of a neighbouring house had enabled them to knock a wall away and provide full catering facilities on the ground floor.

Archie Brooks was in generous mood. They had an excellent dinner and he chatted away amicably, giving them a running commentary on the people at the other tables. Not till the coffee was served was any reference made to their reason for being there.

"Are you sure you won't have a liqueur, Mrs Temple?"

"Quite sure," said Steve.

"What about you, Temple?"

"No, thanks."

"Well, we'll have a cigar anyway." Brooks reached one hand backwards to interrupt a passing waiter. "Robert, fetch us a couple of decent cigars, will you?"

Temple felt it was time to broach the matter uppermost in his mind. "Did Sir Graham tell you why we wanted to come here tonight?"

"He said you wanted to see Chris Boyer. I can't imagine why."

"Do you know him well?" Steve asked. Moira and her fiancé had come into the restaurant late and were sitting at a table across the room. She could see Chris Boyer in profile and could not help being fascinated by his good looks.

"Vaguely. I know everybody vaguely, Mrs Temple, that's my job."

"What exactly is your job?"

Brooks raised his eyebrows at Temple's question. "Didn't Sir Graham tell you?"

"No."

"Then I should ask him," said Brooks, smiling pleasantly. "You see Chris Boyer and Moira are over there. Shall I invite him over for a drink?"

"No, that might look a bit obvious. Tell him . . . " But Boyer had seen that they were talking about him and he was well aware that Steve had been watching him. He pushed his chair back, said something to Moira and stood up.

"He's coming over," Steve said, smiling to herself.

Boyer weaved his elegant way between the tables. He made an art of the simple act of walking.

"Hello, Chunky, how are you?"

"Fine thanks. I'd like you to meet some friends of mine – Mr and Mrs Temple. Chris Boyer."

"Mr Temple and I have already met." Boyer merely glanced at Temple then turned the full charm of his smile on Steve. "But this is an unexpected pleasure, Mrs Temple."

"Now, now Chris, you needn't switch on the charm. I've already warned Mrs Temple you're an out and out Casanova."

"I take that as a compliment." Boyer was still looking at Steve. "Perhaps you'd honour me with a dance when you've finished your dinner – if Mr Temple doesn't mind."

"Thank you, I should love to," said Steve. Then she added "We were awfully sorry to read about your friend."

"What friend?"

"The one you had an appointment with here."

"I'm afraid I don't understand."

"It was in the evening papers. He was knocked down by a taxi outside Harridge's."

Boyer's smile had given way to a frown. "I don't know what you are talking about. I had no appointment this evening, except with Moira."

"There must be some mistake. I thought this man was a friend of yours. His name was Mark Kendell."

"I've never heard of him," Boyer said, annoyed at Steve's persistence. "Who gave you the idea he was a friend of mine?"

"Oh, something my husband said." Steve glanced at Temple, who was absorbed in cutting his cigar. "I must have misunderstood him."

"I'm afraid you must have done," said Boyer coldly. "And now if you'll excuse me."

"Somehow, Steve," Temple remarked, as he watched

Boyer make his way back to Moira, "I doubt very much whether you'll be having that dance."

"I doubt it too," smiled Steve.

"Do you think he was telling the truth?"

"Yes, I do, Paul. He may be a smoothie but I don't think he was lying."

"You could be wrong." Brooks applied a match to his cigar. "Old Chris is an accomplished liar. He lies even better than he dances." He studied the glowing ash appreciatively. "By the way, Sir Graham told me to give you a message. You know those notes, the ones in the attaché case?"

Temple nodded.

"They were counterfeit. Darned good counterfeit too. Personally I couldn't tell the difference."

"Did Sir Graham tell you about Kendell – about what happened?"

"Yes. As a matter of fact I knew him. He used to be an artist with one of the big advertising agencies. Temperamental sort of chap from what I remember."

"How well did you know him?"

"Oh vaguely. Very vaguely." Brooks waved his cigar in a gesture that depicted vagueness. Then he looked at his watch, saw with a shock what the time was.

"I say, look here, Temple – it's a quarter to twelve, would you mind terribly if we broke up the party?"

"No, of course not. I was going to suggest that we made a move."

"Have you got a date, Mr Brooks?" Steve asked, amused by Chunky's pantomime.

"Good Lord, no! Only I promised to pop round and see my sister. She's got a flat just round the corner."

"Your sister?" Steve echoed, on the verge of laughter.

"Yes." Chunky laughed and gave Steve a look. "She's been my sister for years. But Temple, you two don't have to leave. Why not stay and enjoy yourselves?"

"Excuse me, sir." Robert had been respectfully waiting for a gap in the conversation.

"Yes, what is it, Robert?"

"There's a telephone call for Mrs Temple, sir."

"For me?"

"Yes, madam."

"Are you sure it isn't for Mr Temple?"

"Quite sure, sir. The gentleman particularly asked for Mrs Temple. He refused to give his name, sir."

Puzzled by the summons, Steve stood up. "Yes, all right, I'll take it."

"I'll come with you, dear." Temple had risen too. "Goodbye, Brooks. Thanks for the dinner."

"Delighted, old boy." Brooks responded with a cheery wave "Goodbye, Mrs Temple. See you again sometime, I hope."

Steve and Temple both managed to squeeze into the telephone booth near the cloakroom. Even with the door closed they could hear the beat from the amplifiers in the basement.

"Shall I take it?" Steve asked nervously.

"Yes, of course."

Steve lifted the receiver and a few seconds later the club switchboard put the outside call through.

"Hello, is that Mrs Temple?"

"Yes."

"This is George Kelly here. Do you remember me?" Temple nodded, he recognised the nasal twang of Sam Portland's secretary. "We met on the boat coming over from the States."

"Yes, of course I remember you. You're Mr Portland's secretary."

"I *was* his secretary. Yes, you've got the right guy all right. Mrs Temple, listen. There's something I want to say to you."

"Well, I'm listening, Mr Kelly."

"Now, don't take this wrong. This isn't a melodramatic warning, it's a nice friendly piece of advice. I took a liking to that husband of yours, Mrs Temple. He looks a pretty regular guy."

"Well, I think so." Steve smiled at her husband. "Of course, I may be prejudiced."

"Regular guys like that should be taken care of, you know. They shouldn't be allowed to go around pushing their noses into affairs which don't concern them."

"What do you mean?"

"Tell your husband to keep out of this Madison case. If he doesn't he's going to get mixed up with a bunch of very unpleasant customers." Kelly gave his high-pitched laugh. "I know, I happen to be one of them."

"I don't think you're unpleasant, Mr Kelly," Steve replied, "a little stupid perhaps, but not unpleasant."

"You don't know me, baby. Let's hope you don't get to know me. Remember what I've told you. You have a word with that husband of yours. If he's smart, he'll catch on."

"Mr Kelly, just supposing your wife told . . . "

"I haven't got a wife, honey."

Steve was angry at being subjected to such a crude and banal threat. Her voice hardened. "Well, supposing you had a wife and supposing you were mixed up in the Madison case and supposing she told you to keep your nose out of it. What would you do, Mr Kelly?"

Kelly paused before answering and when he did so there was no trace of humour in his voice.

"I'd take a slow boat to China." Then he rang off. Steve replaced the receiver.

"Could you hear what he was saying?"

"Yes."

"What did you make of it?"

"I don't know, but one thing struck me. Did you notice, Steve? He said 'Tell your husband to keep out of this Madison case.' Not Portland case – but Madison. Yet when I spoke to Kelly on the boat he said he'd never even heard of Madison."

"Yes, but who is Madison? If Portland was telling the truth and he's a private detective, he shouldn't be difficult to find."

Temple opened the door of the booth, which had become stiflingly hot. The din of a hundred voices competing with the disco seemed louder than ever.

"Well, the Yard can't find him. Sir Graham's been on his track for almost a week now."

"There's another thing, Paul. How did Kelly know we were here?"

Temple did not answer that question. He was leading the way towards the stairs that led to the cellar.

"Where are we going?"

"To do some dancing. Chunky told us to stay and enjoy ourselves."

The small oval of dancing space was not very crowded

and they were able to slip in quite easily among the couples. Moira Portland and Chris Boyer were already on the floor. When the master of ceremonies put on the number that was top of the pops, Moira and her partner became galvanised. Gradually the other couples fell away, leaving them space to perform what was really a highly professional exhibition. Moira was inspired by Chris's expertise. She became a completely different person from the petulant girl who had made fun of Hubert Greene.

But the amplification and the blaze of coloured lights was too much for Steve. She mouthed at Temple, "I've had enough of this." He took the hint and followed her up the stairs. Oblivious to everybody else, Chris and Moira went on gyrating.

Temple had parked his car down a side street about a hundred yards from the club. Steve gripped his arm tight as they walked west up the King's Road. Traffic was still heavy and there were bands of youths who had stayed in the pubs till the last moment.

Steve was relieved when they turned into the comparatively dark and deserted side street.

"Paul, I've been thinking about Hubert Greene. Do you think he simply invented that story about Madison to get Portland over here?"

"According to Greene he'd plenty of excuses for getting Portland over here."

"His daughter, for instance? What did you think of Moira Portland?"

"I don't know what to think of her. She's either what Hubert Greene says she is, the spoilt daughter of a millionaire or . . . she's putting on a very good act."

"Well, I can't say I like her fiancé – although he dances like an angel. Paul, you left your side-lights on!"

They had reached the car. Temple frowned, reaching in his pocket for the keys. He moved out into the road, towards the driver's side. He was about to insert the key in the lock when he froze.

"That's funny, I could have sworn . . . "

"What is it?"

"Steve, listen."

Then Steve heard it too, a low gasping moan from somewhere inside the car. She pressed her face against the glass of the back window. It was misted by condensation on the inside.

"There's someone on the floor in the back. I can't quite . . . "

Temple had turned his key to operate the central locking system. He ran round to Steve's side, opened the back door. As he did so he felt the weight pushing against it. A body slithered out. The head struck Steve's foot and inert arms slumped in the gutter. The legs were still trapped behind the front seat. The interior light had automatically gone on and its ray illuminated the ghastly upturned face.

"Paul! It's Archie Brooks! What's happened?"

"Don't touch him, Steve." Temple had seen the blood-stained clothing. He guessed that there had been several stab wounds. The awful pallor of Brooks' face showed that he had lost a great deal of blood. "Run back to the club and phone for an ambulance. Find out if there's a doctor—"

"No!" The word came from the injured man. "Too late . . . I . . ." Brooks' head rolled with the effort to speak.

"Quick, Steve!"

"No, wait!" Temple knelt on the pavement his ear close to Brooks. "Must tell you . . . man was killed . . . Mark—!"

"Mark Kendell? Yes, go on!"

"Thought—" Brooks was fighting pain, weakness, lack of breath. "Thought he had a meeting . . . Chris Boyer?"

"That's what we thought. It was in his diary. Appointment with C.B."

"Not Chris Boyer . . ." The thing that Steve would never be able to erase from her mind was the terrible effigy of a grin that twisted the dying man's mouth.

"Brooks . . . everybody . . . calls me Chunky . . . "

Temple did not try to feel for his heart or check his pulse. He'd seen death often enough to recognise its countenance. He straightened up.

"He's dead, Paul?"

Temple nodded, unable to speak.

"Paul, how did they get into the car – if it was locked?"

Temple did not answer. He was still staring down at the bloodstained bundle of clothing that had so recently been Chunky Brooks. There was something frightening about the way he was lying, arms and legs in the car, head still in the gutter. The voices of a group of people who had turned into the street from the King's Road echoed from the walls on the opposite side. Temple got his hands under Brooks' armpits and heaved the upper part of his body back into the car. He held it with one hand, the head lolling against his forearms, and managed to close the door on it. The light went out.

"I broke my rule and left my keys in the pocket of my overcoat while we were in the club." He was panting from the effort of moving the dead weight. "Steve, you know Sir Graham's number. Go back to the Manila and 'phone him. Tell him exactly what's happened. If you can't reach him get through to the Yard. Then take a taxi back to the . . . What is it? What are you looking for?"

Steve had stooped. Her hand was groping over the edge of the kerb. Just before the light went out she had seen something glinting in the gutter. It had been hidden by Chunky's body. She straightened up and wiped the dirt off the object she had found. By the dim light of the street lamps she could just see that it was one of the large old-fashioned pennies.

"What is it?" Temple asked again.

Silently she handed it to him. He opened the front door of the car to activate the interior light. The large penny lay on the palm of his hand, the head of George VI uppermost. It had been pierced so that it could be attached to a key-ring. He turned it over to peer at the date.

"1952."

3   Eileen

"Another cup of coffee, Sir Graham?"

"Yes, Steve, if I may."

Forbes handed his cup over to Steve, who refilled it. The three of them were in the Temples' sitting-room. Steve had pulled back the curtains to admit the grey light of dawn. There had been no question of sleep for the Temples that night. It had been half past five before the police car dropped them off in Eaton Square. Forbes had arrived just as a sleepy Charlie rustled up a large jug of strong coffee.

"I'm very concerned about Brooks, Temple." Forbes was restlessly pacing the room. "I'd always looked upon him as being completely trustworthy. Admittedly he was an extravagant sort of person, even inclined to overstep the mark so far as expenses were concerned, but we never doubted his integrity."

Temple glanced at Steve and smiled. They'd had a taste of Chunky's generosity. "Well, I can only tell you what he said, Sir Graham."

"He told you that he had an appointment with Mark Kendell, that he was the C.B. referred to in the diary?" Forbes was still reluctant to accept the facts Temple had given him.

"There's no question about it, Sir Graham," Steve confirmed. "I heard it as well as Paul."

"What exactly did Brooks do?" Temple asked. "Was he attached to the CID?"

"Yes. He had rather a curious position, Temple. He started with us about seven or eight years ago. He had quite an unimportant job to start with and then one day Superintendent Henson asked him to investigate the activities of a certain night club. We'd had our suspicions about this particular club and we wanted a detailed report of what was going on behind the scenes. Brooks got it for us – in fact, he put in a first rate report. Ever since then we've used him almost exclusively as a contact, a sort of . . . "

"Our man in London?"

"Exactly. I'd rather taken to Brooks, Temple. I'm very sad this has happened."

"I can understand that, but it does rather look as if he was mixed up in this affair, doesn't it?"

"Yes, it does," Forbes agreed, still perturbed. "You know, Temple, I may be dense but I don't quite see how all these pieces fit together. Take this man Kendell for instance. Kendell was quite obviously mixed up in the counterfeit racket and yet it was Kendell who broke into your flat. Now why on earth should he do that? What was he looking for? Was it the watch-chain or something else?"

Outside in the hall the front door buzzer sounded. Steve went to answer it. Charlie had gone back to bed again to complete his interrupted night's sleep.

"Shall I tell you what I think, Sir Graham? This Portland affair, the murder of Archie Brooks, and this business about the watch-chain and the 1952 penny are part and parcel of the same case."

"You think it's all mixed up with the counterfeit racket?"

"I do, and I'm convinced that you'll never smash that racket until you've solved the mystery of the penny and revealed the identity of Madison. What is it, darling?"

Steve had appeared at the doorway, masking the person who was waiting in the hall.

"It's Chief Inspector James."

"Show him in, Steve." Temple went to meet the CID man who was hesitating to break in on a conversation between his chief and the novelist. "Come in, Inspector," he welcomed him warmly. "Sir Graham's here."

Chief Inspector James was a small, compact man with features which appeared to have been attracted towards the centre of his face. Temple guessed that he must have barely passed the height qualification for the Metropolitan Police. He seemed a little old to have risen no higher than the rank of Chief Inspector. Perhaps that had something to do with his almost aggressively wary manner. He was very dark and an early morning shadow of stubble ringed his jaw.

"Good morning, sir." He made a point of greeting Forbes first, then turned a shuttered face towards his host. "Good morning, Mr Temple. I don't think we've met before, sir."

"No, I don't think we have. Can I get you a coffee, Inspector?"

"No, thank you." James declined with the firmness of a man who does not permit himself frivolous luxuries.

"Well, have you finished?" Forbes asked him.

"We've finished with the car, sir. It's been photographed from more angles than Marilyn Monroe."

"Did you find anything?"

"No dabs, sir. We've sent some stuff to forensic, including the penny, and will just have to wait and see if they come up with anything."

"How far is the club from where the car was parked?"

"About fifty yards, Sir Graham. The street's a cul-de-sac. I can't imagine what poor old Chunky was doing down there."

"Was Brooks a friend of yours, Inspector?" Temple intervened.

"I don't think I'd exactly call him a friend, sir." James permitted himself a faint smile. "I knew him a little better than most people at the Yard because we once did a double act together at a police concert."

"What did you do, James?" Forbes asked with a hint of banter. "Song and dance?"

"No, sir. I did impersonations. Brooks was the song and dance man. And very good he was too." James shook his head and for once allowed some emotion to stir his features. "It's a damn shame about Brooks, sir."

Forbes nodded, meeting the junior man's eyes.

"Have you any idea what time he left the Manila?" Temple asked.

"He must have left while you and Mrs Temple were in the telephone box, sir. The bouncer said he saw you leave about half an hour after Brooks."

"He told us he intended to drop in and see his sister," Steve said. "Whether he was pulling our legs or not I don't know."

"Brooks hadn't got a sister, Mrs Temple," James told her, straight-faced. "He was an only child. He'd plenty of lady friends though – that's probably what he meant."

"Where did he live, James?"

"He had a flat in Whitedown Gardens, Sir Graham.

That's just off the Cromwell Road. As a matter of fact I'm on my way there now."

"Would you mind if I went along with you, Inspector?"

"Well . . ." James was taken aback at Temple's request and for a split second his suspicion of an investigator outside the Force showed in his eyes.

"Yes, that's all right, James," said Forbes, blithely over-riding the implied refusal.

"If you say so, sir." James inclined his head as a sign of his obedience to his Chief's command.

"Fine, I'll get my things." Temple spoke cheerily, though James' reluctance had not been lost on him. "Oh, you've got a car, I take it? I'm without mine till you people have finished with it."

"Yes, Mr Temple. I do have a car."

Inevitably the lift was already in use. The overhead indicator showed that it had just reached the ground floor. Forbes, James and Temple watched it impatiently. At last the G gave way to a 1 and then a 2.

"It's coming," Temple murmured.

A moment later the lift doors opened. In deference James insisted on the other two preceding him. He had just squeezed in after them when the automatic doors closed.

"Which button do I press?" James was peering at the array of touch switches.

"G," said Temple. "It's the last but one."

Before James' finger had reached the button the lift jerked into movement.

"What have I done?"

"It's all right, Inspector." Temple laughed. "It must be someone on the floor above."

The lift ascended one floor and the doors opened. On the landing outside was standing a tall man of about thirty with a friendly face and strikingly blonde hair.

"Oh! I beg your pardon!" he exclaimed at the sight of the three men. "I thought the lift was free."

"That's all right." Temple put an arm out to prevent the lift door closing. "You just caught us in time."

"Please?"

"We were just going down. There's room for one more."

The tall man squeezed in, still a little embarrassed.

"Do you want the ground floor?"

"If you please."

The doors closed. This time James got the right button and the floor of the lift dropped away. It struck Temple that the stranger had probably bathed quite recently since he smelt of bath essence, soap and after-shave. His slight accent seemed to indicate that he was Nordic, probably from Denmark.

"My name's Temple. Have you taken Major Hartley's flat?"

"Yes, I moved in four or five days ago. The day you returned from America, Mr Temple."

"Oh." Temple was surprised by the man's acumen but encouraged by the friendly smile.

"My name is Dr Elzec."

"We have the flat under yours, doctor. Drop in one evening for a drink. My wife and I would be delighted to see you."

"That is most kind."

"Did you say Dr Elzec, sir?" James had been looking up at the Dane's face.

"Yes," said Elzec, focussing on the much smaller CID man. "But I think we have met somewhere before?"

"That's just what I was thinking," said James.

The lift stopped with a slight jerk and the door opened. With an apologetic gesture Elzec stepped out first, turned to give a slight bow and then walked with long strides out through the front door.

"You know him?" Temple asked, following James and Forbes out of the lift.

"I've seen him somewhere before but I'm dashed if I can place him."

"Elzec," said Forbes. "The name mean anything?"

"No, that's the extraordinary part of it. I don't think the name's Elzec at all, in fact I'm sure it isn't."

"Then what is it?"

"It'll come to me, Sir Graham. Is this the first time you've seen him, Mr Temple?"

"Yes. Apparently he's taken Major Hartley's furnished flat. Hartley's with the Foreign Office. He's been transferred to Washington."

"I wish I could remember where I've seen him." James

shook his head, searching the floor for inspiration. "Elzec. I'm sure that's not the name."

Whitedown Gardens belied it's name. It was a run-down street off North End Road, a few minutes walk from West Kensington Underground station. The houses, once substantial residences, had without exception been converted to flats. Cars were parked nose to tail along the kerb. Some of them appeared abandoned and were covered with leaves and bird droppings. There were no spaces and James double-parked the unnumbered Ford outside number 27.

Temple had done what he could during the short drive to break down the Chief Inspector's resentment at having a well-known crime writer breathing down his neck. James had thawed slightly but the manner in which he led the way up the front steps and hammered on the knocker made it clear that this was his case and Temple was no more than an observer.

A head was poked out of an upstairs window, but no one came to answer the door. James wielded the knocker again.

"I think there's someone coming," Temple murmured.

"Not before time."

"Who lives here, do you know?"

"A chap called Scaley owns the place. Brooks has the top floor."

A heavy bolt was drawn back, a key turned in the lock and a chain rattled. James was standing close to the door, as it opened, ready to jam it with his foot.

"Good morning. I'd like to—"

An angry face had appeared in the gap. It was unshaven and topped by a head of ginger hair.

"What the devil do you think you're doing, man, knocking on the door like that? Why for goodness sakes don't you use the bell?"

"Where's the bell?" said James, wrong-footed right from the start.

"It's right under your nose, man! It's staring you in the face!"

A grubby, stubby finger stabbed the bell push. Deep inside the house a bell shrilled angrily.

"There, you see! It's quite unnecessary to be making all that noise."

The little Welshman was three inches shorter than James but about a yard wider. He'd pulled a pair of trousers over his pyjamas and flung on an old jacket. That he was Welsh was obvious from his speech and intonation.

"Are you Mr Scaley?" James demanded, striving to re-assert his authority.

"I am," defiantly.

"Well, I've come about Mr Brooks."

"Then I wish to goodness you'd have a word with him. Would you mind telling the gentleman to stop his fancy ladies from ringing at all hours? There hasn't been a moment's peace in this house. His phone's been ringing since six o'clock this morning."

"Yes, well don't worry, Mr Scaley – from now on that's a thing of the past."

"What do you mean?"

"I'm afraid Mr Brooks has met with an accident."

"Accident? What sort of an accident?"

"He's dead."

"Why, man, I don't believe it! You're pulling my leg now! It's a joke, isn't it?" Scaley turned to appeal to Temple. "Now tell me it's a joke."

"No, it's not a joke, Mr Scaley," said James. Having dropped his bombshell he felt able to assume his official manner. "I'm Chief Inspector James of Scotland Yard. This is Mr Temple." Scaley blinked at Temple. He'd heard the name before but could not place it. James prompted him gently. "May we come inside?"

Recovering himself Scaley opened the door wide, but still used it to half screen his dishevelled clothing. "Yes, yes of course! Archie Brooks . . . dead!" He was shaking his head and muttering to himself as he closed the door behind him. "Why, man, I can't believe it. Lordy, I just don't believe it."

Temple had understood why James was so sensitive about this case. It was because Sir Graham Forbes had been ready to entertain doubts about Brooks' integrity and Brooks was a colleague of his. If there were going to be revelations about police complicity in a counterfeit racket the Force could handle the inquiry themselves without any assistance from outside.

Accordingly Temple let James deal with the examination of the flat in his own way. While the Chief Inspector went about the business of checking the contents of Brooks' residence – searching for papers, opening the drawers of the desk, riffling through diaries and note books, examining the contents of the bathroom cabinet, nosing out possible secret hiding places – Temple was careful to keep his hands to himself. But he gave his eyes every possible chance.

For such a run-down area the flat was pleasantly furnished and decorated. As a bachelor Brooks did himself well. There were good rugs on the floor of the sitting-room and striking paintings on the walls. A modern music centre plus TV and video stood in one corner and a well stocked cocktail cabinet in the other. The kitchen was small and ill equipped with only the essentials for preparing breakfast. Brooks evidently went out for most meals. His bathroom was stocked not only with masculine toiletries but with bath essences, sprays and eau de toilette more suitable for feminine use. The feature of the bedroom was a large double bed with a full-width mirror instead of a head board. A set of day clothes was neatly draped on a chair – dark suit, shirt, tie, underwear and socks.

James was just feeling under the piles of pants, vests and handkerchiefs in one of the drawers.

Temple said, "He must have come back last night to change before going to the Manila."

"Yes, according to our Welsh friend downstairs he went out about eight." James closed the drawer. "I don't think I'm going to find anything here. The sitting-room's more interesting."

"Find anything of interest?" Temple asked casually, following James through the connecting door.

"Nothing of importance. There's a few letters, a diary and a couple of snapshot albums. I'll take them back to the office."

"Is this the first time you've been here, Inspector?"

"Yes." James looked round him with a certain degree of envy. "Nice place, isn't it?"

The telephone on the desk started to ring. Automatically James moved to answer it.

"Don't touch it, let it ring."

James halted in mid-stride. He frowned at the peremptory command.

"James, you said you could do impersonations. Do you think you could impersonate Brooks?"

"Chunky?" James' face relaxed. "Yes. Yes, I think I could."

"All right, have a shot at it!"

"You mean – you want me to answer the telephone and pretend to be Chunky?"

"Yes, go on. I'll listen in the bedroom on the extension."

Dubious but at the same time tempted by the challenge, James put a hand on the receiver. Temple ran into the bedroom to lift the bedside phone there at the same time.

"Hello? Is that you, Chunky?" A woman's voice, youthful by the sound of it.

"Yes – this is Chunky. Who is that?"

Temple smiled. James' voice was totally different and remarkably like Brooks' excitable, high pitched way of talking.

"Why this is Eileen – who did you think it was?"

"I'm sorry, I didn't recognise your voice."

"You sound different – is anything the matter?"

"No, I was asleep, that's all. Where are you? Where are you speaking from?"

"I'm at home . . . It's all right – he can't hear. He's still in bed, asleep." The voice was sexy, cosy and confiding. "Chunky, listen . . . I found out what you wanted."

"You did?" James was being as economical as possible with words.

"It's tomorrow night."

"Tomorrow night?"

"Yes. Eleven o'clock . . . "

"What?"

"Oh, Chunky darling, do try and listen. I said eleven o'clock . . . "

"Oh, I see," said James, breathing a little heavily with the effort of keeping his voice at an unnaturally high pitch.

"Well, aren't you going to ask me where?"

Obediently James asked, "Where, Eileen?"

There was a short pause, then the caller snapped in a completely different tone of voice, "You're not Chunky!" and the receiver was immediately slammed down.

When Temple came back into the sitting-room James was

still holding the receiver. He put it down slowly and gave Temple an apologetic look.

"I made a mess of that one, I'm afraid."

"No, you didn't. You put up a marvellous show!"

"You think so really?" James was brightening up.

"Of course I do. I'd have taken you for Chunky myself if I had not known."

"Phew! I feel like a piece of chewed string. She was just going to give me the vital bit of information, you know, when I blew it." James sighed.

"They probably had some pet word. You couldn't know that."

"I was dying to ask her who she was." James chuckled "Eileen. Eileen who, Temple? Sexy voice, eh?" James grinned. All of a sudden the barrier between them was down.

"Yes. You may find it if you've a list of 'phone numbers there. I wonder if Scaley knows her?"

"There's just a chance that he might. Come on. Let's go down and ask him."

But Owen Scaley could recall no girl-friend of that name. There was a Phyllis, a Dora, a Pat, a Samantha – but no Eileen.

"Will you be reporting to Sir Graham about that 'phone call?" James asked as they were getting into the police car.

Temple looked him in the eye. "No, I won't. It's your report, Inspector."

James nodded and gave Temple a pat on the shoulder. Temple knew he had made a friend.

"Pass the toast, Paul."

"Mm?"

"I said, pass the toast, darling."

"Oh! Sorry."

"You seem very quiet."

Temple lowered the newspaper. He'd not really been reading it, using it more as a screen to hide behind. "What do you mean, quiet? Of course I'm quiet! What do you expect me to be like? It's eleven o'clock and I'm only just having breakfast."

"That makes two of us. I thought you'd be pleased I waited for you."

Temple sighed and looked contrite. "I'm annoyed with myself, Steve."

"Annoyed? What are you annoyed with yourself about?"

The little storm in a teacup had passed. Like any married couple who had a perfect and sympathetic understanding the Temples sometimes had these minor tiffs. Both of them knew that sometimes they had to let off steam and it was better to do it on someone who would quickly forgive and forget.

"I jumped to conclusions, darling. The wrong conclusions."

"About Archie Brooks?"

"Yes."

"Yes," Steve allowed herself a private smile, "I thought you had."

"Why – what did you think?" said Temple, peering round the side of the paper.

"I thought Brooks was mixed up in this business but I felt sure he was on the right side."

"What made you so sure?"

"Oh, just intuition," said Steve with a lift of the chin.

"Oh, by Timothy!" Temple lowered the paper with mock apprehension. "Don't tell me that good old intuition's on the war-path again!"

"Well, the way things are at the moment you can certainly do with it!"

"By the way, Steve, have you seen the young fellow who's taken the flat above?"

"Yes, I caught a glimpse of him yesterday morning. They say he's taken it on a six month lease. Supposed to be paying five hundred a week."

"Five hundred a week! By Timothy, Dr Elzec must have a pretty flourishing practice!"

"Is he a doctor?"

"Well, he said he was. I met him in the lift when I went down with the Chief Inspector. As a matter of fact James thought he recognised him."

"He looks a pleasant sort of person, but he certainly doesn't look like a doctor."

"He'll probably turn out to be an osteopath or a chiropractor or a masseur or something. Doctors come in all shapes and sizes these days. I've asked him to drop in for a drink one evening."

Out in the hall the front door buzzer sounded.

"Darling, answer that," Steve pleaded. "I can't go like this."

"Where's Charlie?"

"He's gone shopping."

Temple gave Steve time to hurry through to the bedroom before he went to open the door.

Hubert Greene was wearing a light check shower proof coat over his business suit and was already holding his wide-brimmed hat in his hand.

"Why, hello, Greene!"

"Hello, Temple! Sorry if I've interrupted anything."

"No, as a matter of fact I'm just having breakfast. But do come in!"

Greene stepped across the doormat into the hall. His quick eyes checked the hats and coats on the stand.

"It's a bit of an impertinence dropping in like this, but I did rather want to see you and since I was passing the door I thought I might as well . . . "

"It's not an impertinence at all," said Temple, making a great effort to be civil. "Delighted to see you. Would you like some coffee?"

"No, thank you."

"Well, let me take your things, and come on in."

"No, I won't keep you a minute, Temple. As a matter of fact I only dropped in because – well – I'd like you and Mrs Temple to come down to my place for the weekend. Mrs Portland, Moira and George Kelly are coming down. We'd like you and Mrs Temple to join us."

"Well, I don't know." Temple had been taken by surprise. He somehow felt that Greene's sudden friendliness was not sincere. "This weekend happens to be rather awkward. You see, we – er – we did think of . . . "

"It's awfully difficult to think of excuses, isn't it?" Greene's smile was polite. "Especially on the spur of the moment."

"It's not that, but—" Temple abandoned all pretence at diplomacy and asked bluntly, "Mr Greene, why are you inviting my wife and I for the weekend? Let's face it, we're not exactly friends – are we – barely acquaintances?"

"Shall I be frank, Temple?" Greene said, unruffled.

"I should prefer it."

"The very first time I met you, down at Southampton, I said to myself, now there's a man I would really like to get to know. An intellectual but at the same time a man of action. It's a combination I've always admired, Mr Temple."

"I thought we were going to be frank with each other."

"What do you mean!" asked Greene, all innocence.

"The first time you met me you thought I was a confounded nuisance. So far as you were concerned I was an unmitigated bore pushing my nose into an affair which didn't concern me."

"Was that the impression I gave you?"

"I'm afraid it was."

Greene gave a wry laugh and scratched the side of his nose. Then he shrugged, resigning himself to tell the real reason for his visit.

"Well, if you must know, I particularly want Moira Portland to come down to my house this weekend. We've quite a lot of family business to discuss and without Moira the whole thing would be quite pointless."

"Yes, you told me that last night, you said she wouldn't accept your invitation unless you included the boyfriend."

"Moira telephoned me this morning, she said we could expect her on one condition."

"What was that?"

"That you and Mrs Temple were invited."

"But why on earth should Moira Portland insist that my wife and I spend the weekend with you? We barely know the girl. As a matter of fact my wife doesn't know her, she didn't even meet her last night at the Manila."

"Moira's a strange girl. A very determined one too. If you don't accept the invitation I doubt very much if I shall see her."

Greene turned his head at the sound of a key in the door. Charlie came in, weighed down with carrier bags. He was wearing a battered old mackintosh and had a transparent plastic cowl over his head to keep the rain off his bald patch. He did not see the two men in the hall till he had extracted his key and closed the door.

"Oh!" with a little start. "Beg pardon, Mr Temple, I didn't know . . . "

Greene watched in amazement while the apparition crossed the hall and disappeared into the kitchen.

"I'm sorry, Greene," Temple said "Both my wife and I have other plans."

"Well—" Greene sighed. "I thought I'd give it a try."

"Why does Miss Portland want us anyway?" Temple asked, curious.

"I asked her that. She said that if you came down for the weekend she'd feel quite sure that nothing unfortunate would happen."

"Nothing unfortunate?"

"Oh, didn't I tell you? Moira's under the impression that her life's in danger. Apparently she's been under that impression for weeks now. It's almost a joke at the office."

"Do you think her life's in danger?"

"Why, of course not!" Greene laughed, scoffing at the idea. "Why should it be?"

Temple had been watching him, not only his face but his body language. With a complete change of mood he suddenly asked. "Where is your place, Greene?"

"It's just outside Leatherhead. Quite a nice little place. As a matter of fact I've got about a hundred acres."

"It does sound a nice little place," Temple agreed dryly.

"Temple, I'm sorry to have issued this invitation in such an unorthodox manner, but the fact of the matter is I am in rather a hole." Greene was rotating his hat in his hands. "I've got to please Mrs Portland and at the same time keep on friendly terms with Moira. It's not easy."

"I'm quite sure it isn't. And how does George Kelly fit into the picture?"

"Well, as you know, Kelly was Portland's secretary. He now appears to have taken on the job of financial adviser to Mrs Portland. In short, he's making a damn nuisance of himself."

Temple laughed. "It does sound a jolly little house-party."

"It certainly could do with an up-lift, if that's what you mean."

"What do they call your place?"

"It's called 'Brown Acres'. It's just off the main road the other side of Leatherhead." Greene paused, beginning to realise the reason for these questions. "Why?"

"You can expect us on Saturday. We'll be there in time for lunch."

70

"Well, that's damned sporting of you, Temple! I appreciate it." The tension and worry had gone out of Greene's face. "What made you change your mind?"

Temple smiled. "Well, the first time I saw you at Southampton, Mr Greene, I said to myself – now, there's a man I would really like to get to know . . . "

'Brown Acres' was an important enough property to be marked on the large-scale Ordnance Survey map. With Steve doing the map-reading the Temples had no problem in finding it. The digital clock was just coming up to twelve forty-five when Paul turned the Jaguar in through a pair of fine wrought-iron gates. The house stood in the middle of its hundred acres of parkland. The approach was through an avenue lined with beech trees, which curved round a lake and then climbed the hill on which it stood. It was a fine, well-proportioned Georgian residence with a porticoed entrance and a terrace overlooking the lawns on the southern side. Two cars already stood on the broad sweep of gravel below the triple row of windows, one row being elegant dormers protruding from the roof. Temple was glad he had chosen the Jaguar in preference to Steve's Mazda coupé. The XJS which had been photographed from as many angles as Marilyn Monroe rubbed shoulders more easily with the Mercedes SLR and the Porsche 924 already parked beside the manicured edge of the lawn.

Hubert Greene must have heard the crunch of wheels on gravel, for he had come out of the house before they had time to undo their seat-belts and step out. He was followed by a small, dark man in a white coat. Greene himself was in country gentleman's gear – brown corduroys, an open-necked shirt, cashmere cardigan and buckskin shoes.

"Hello, Temple! Welcome to 'Brown Acres'!"

"I'm afraid we're a little on the late side, Greene." Temple apologised, stretching his shoulders back. "We didn't leave Town till after eleven."

"Nonsense! You're in perfect time!" Greene said warmly. He beamed at Steve. "Delighted to see you, Mrs Temple. Leave your things in the car, Temple, my man will take care of them."

"Oh, thank you. My word, it's a nice place you've got here."

Temple turned to admire the view, which was enhanced by the house's position on a hill. With its lake and vistas through clumps of trees 'Brown Acres' had the flavour of a Capability Brown creation.

"I think you'll like it," Greene said, with assumed modesty.

He led the way up the three stone steps. Temple had given 'my man' the car keys and he was opening the boot.

"Have all the guests arrived?"

"Yes, they're all here, including Moira. I'm glad to say she's behaving herself for a change."

Steve had paused to admire the view to southward. "What a lovely terrace!"

"Do you like it?" Pleased, Greene stopped to share the enjoyment with her. "The lake adds a lot to the view. There's a local superstition that it's bottomless but we haven't tried to prove it!"

"I think it's heavenly!"

"I'm quite proud of 'Brown Acres', Mrs Temple. Be a pleasure to show you round. Would you like to go to your rooms straight away or would you care for a drink first?"

Greene was a much more confident and relaxed person on his own territory and friendly to the point of effusiveness. Making the decision for them, he gave a broad grin and took Steve by the arm. "Come along, let's join the others on the terrace. I am sure you're both dying for a drink."

The terrace was reached through a large drawing-room to the right of the hall. The windows were tall and walking through it Steve could see across the terrace to the lawn, trees and sky beyond.

Three people were already out there, sitting on white upholstered garden chairs round a white metal table. The raucous voice of George Kelly drifted through the french windows.

"Why, you're crazy, Stella! How can you say Americans haven't got a sense of humour? Would you say Thurber hadn't got a sense of humour? Or George Kaufman? Or Bob Hope? Now, you take the Marx Brothers . . . "

"No, darling, you take the Marx brothers!" said a woman. Steve recognised the voice of Stella Portland. The trio laughed at her dry comment.

"Are you still lecturing, George?" Hubert chided Portland's erstwhile secretary.

Kelly twisted round to make some rejoinder. "Stella's just had the nerve to tell us that . . . " He stopped at the sight of Steve.

"Why, hello, Mrs Temple!" He rose from his chair. "How are you?"

"Good morning, Mr Kelly," said Steve, her voice as cool as her smile.

"Good morning, Kelly!" Temple's cordial greeting broke a moment of possible tension. "How are you?"

"I'm fine." Kelly gestured towards Mrs Portland, who had turned in her chair to smile at the newcomers. "I guess you know Stella."

"Yes, of course."

Hubert Greene came forward to relieve Kelly of the introductions.

"I don't think you've met my wife, have you, Temple? Darling, this is Mr and Mrs Temple."

The young woman who rose from her chair in a lithe movement was in her late twenties. She wore a deceptively simple white dress which emphasised her dark hair and sun-tanned skin. She had long, shapely legs and an excellent figure.

"Hello, Mrs Temple, delighted to meet you. It's awfully nice of you both to join us for the weekend." Her voice was low and musical with a quality which Temple labelled in his mind as sultry.

"It's awfully nice of you to ask us," Steve echoed, taking the proffered hand.

"We've been looking forward to it," said Temple.

"Do sit down, Mrs Temple." Mrs Greene pulled up an extra chair. Steve sat down, crossed her legs, and looked up to meet Temple's eye. "What would you like to drink?"

"May I have a dry Martini?"

"Yes, of course. Mr Temple?"

Temple had heard the question but he did not answer. It was as if he were listening for something, perhaps the screech of a water-hen on the lake. Then he collected himself. "A . . . scotch – with water, no ice."

"A man after my own heart," Hubert Greene approved.

"Isn't it a heavenly view, darling?" said Steve, grasping at conversational straws. She could see that it was going to be a sticky weekend.

"Do you like it?" Mrs Greene had sat down again, arranging her full skirt over her knees.

"Oh, I think it's wonderful, Mrs Greene."

Hubert's wife leant forward to touch Steve's arm in a friendly gesture. "Oh, please – not Mrs Greene."

"For some obscure reason my wife dislikes being called Mrs Greene." Busy at the drinks trolley, Hubert spoke over his shoulder with just a slight touch of sarcasm. "I've never discovered why."

"Darling, don't be silly!"

"But it's true, my dear!"

"Nonsense! None of my friends call me Mrs Greene, you know that! It's always Eileen."

4   Hubert Greene Entertains

There was an awkward silence while Hubert Greene poured out the drinks, making quite sure he knew exactly what Paul and Steve wanted. George Kelly ostentatiously held his glass upside down but Hubert ignored the hint. It was Stella who broke the ice.

"Did you have a pleasant journey, Mrs Temple?"

"If you overlook the fact that we were stuck in a traffic jam for twenty minutes outside Kingston, we had a very pleasant journey."

In the polite laughter that greeted her remark Steve turned to Kelly. "I suppose all this is quite new to you, Mr Kelly?"

"What do you mean – the scotch?" Kelly asked, deliberately misunderstanding her.

"No, I mean the countryside."

"Yeah. Kind of takes a bit of getting used to. I like it though." He waved a hand at the parkland. A man and a woman had just come into sight at the bottom of the banded lawn, walking arm in arm. "I like all this green stuff."

Temple asked, "Is this the first time you've been over here?"

"Yeah. I nearly came over with the Cody Boys in '74 but I changed my mind at the last moment. Wish I hadn't now, it might have been fun."

"Who are the Cody boys?" Eileen had not heard this one before.

"It was a circus outfit. And boy did we travel! We toured every state in the Union."

"Don't tell me you were the bare-backed rider, George." Eileen said, still ribbing him.

"Well, I wasn't the bearded lady." This time Kelly did raise a laugh. "I was a sort of general factotum. Chief handyman. I started the outfit with a knife-throwing act – and boy was it corny!"

"You mean – you used to throw knives!" Steve exclaimed,

looking with disbelief at the unsteady Kelly.

"That's right. You know the sort of thing, you've seen it thousands of times. A gal stands up against a door in her scanties and some phoney-looking character throws a lot of knives at her." Rather expertly Kelly mimed the act of throwing knives. "If it's a good act the knives just miss, if they don't – well – you're pretty soon out of business."

"Was that what happened to your act, Mr Kelly?"

"Yeah, Mrs Temple. We folded. I was no good. I couldn't get near the gal – I was too darned scared. One night I missed the gal, the door and every goddam thing!" Kelly stared with real sadness into his empty glass. "I just wasn't cut out for show business."

"What were you cut out for, George?" Hubert asked maliciously.

"Why, didn't you know?" Kelly accepted the cue gratefully. "I'm a financial wizard."

Now that they were nearer, Temple recognised the couple coming up the steps as Moira Portland and the gregarious Chris Boyer. They unlinked arms as they came onto the terrace. Moira was fresh-faced and more subdued than she had been in the Manila Club but still obviously besotted by her fiancé.

"Hello, Moira!" Hubert said in a tone of mock surprise. "Where have you been?"

"We've been for a walk. Any objections, Hubert?"

"No, of course not, but I wanted you to meet Mr and Mrs Temple."

"We've met." Moira's expression was non-commital. "We met at the Manila."

"I don't think you've met my wife, Miss Portland," Temple corrected her.

Moira made no move to shake hands. She stayed close to Chris Boyer. "Hello, there."

"Hello there!" Steve responded, true as an echo.

"Mrs Temple," Eileen interposed swiftly. "May I introduce Mr Boyer – Chris to us."

"Oh, we're old friends, aren't we, Mrs Temple?" said Boyer, smiling.

"Well, it's nice of you to say so. After the way I quizzed you the other night I'm surprised we're even on speaking terms!"

"Oh, Chris is used to that sort of thing," said Moira lovingly. "I'm the world's worst nagger, aren't I, sweetie?"

"Positively the world's worst!" Boyer agreed.

"You are rotten, Chris!" said Moira, angry at not being contradicted.

"Come along, Mrs Temple." Eileen rose from her chair, "Let me show you to your room."

"Would you like a drink, Moira?" Hubert was asking.

"Yes, I'll have a vodka and Dubonnet."

"What about you, Boyer?"

"Have you a gin and dry Martini?"

Kelly was holding out his glass as Paul and Steve followed Eileen through the french windows. "Have I your permission to have another scotch, Stella?"

"No, George. I think you've had quite enough for one morning."

"Oh, go on. Let the poor fellow have a drink," said Hubert, laughing. "It won't do him any harm. You won't start throwing knives at us, will you, George?"

"Not if you're nice to me I won't."

Eileen Greene led Temple and Steve through the spacious hall and up a broad, curving staircase to the first floor. They followed her along a creaking corridor to the south bedroom. It was evidently the best guest bedroom, with its own bathroom en-suite. The windows looked out over the front of the house towards the lake.

Steve was surprised by the furniture and decoration. It did not seem to be Hubert Greene's style at all. Many of the pieces were antiques and the pictures, curtains and carpets had that used and slightly time-weathered elegance that you find in English stately homes.

Their suitcases had been put on the beds but not unpacked.

"I think you'll be comfortable, Mrs Temple. If there's anything you'd like just let me know."

"It's a lovely room, isn't it, Paul?"

"Delightful. I was just admiring the view. You seem to be able to see for miles."

Eileen walked to the window to gaze affectionately at the vista.

"Yes, I remember when I was a little girl we used to climb onto the roof and stay there for hours on end. We used to have picnics up there in the summer." She turned, smiling nostalgically. "On a clear day you could see right across the country."

"How long have you been here, Mrs Greene?"

"Well, off and on, I suppose I've been here all my life. You see, the house belonged to my father – Lord Dalesdon. He died in 1983. After he died I shut the house up for a short time and went abroad. As a matter of fact I was in Naples when I met Hubert."

"When was that?"

"That was just over two years ago."

"This house wasn't always called 'Brown Acres', was it?"

"No, good gracious, no! It's really Dalesdon Hall. It's been Dalesdon Hall for generations. For some obscure reason my husband suddenly took it into his head to change the name to 'Brown Acres' . . . " A wistful smile shadowed her face. "I've never discovered why."

"Mrs Greene . . ." Temple began. "Oh, I'm sorry. I forgot, you don't like to be called that."

She had been about to leave them but now turned back. Steve sensed that despite her position as mistress of a fine house she felt a need to talk, to make new friends. "What were you going to say?"

"I was going to ask you a question – rather a personal question, I'm afraid."

"That's all right, Mr Temple. Please go on."

"Was Archie Brooks a friend of yours?"

"Archie Brooks?" Eileen was not practised at concealing her feelings. It was obvious the name had registered with her.

"Yes."

"I'm afraid I've never heard of anyone called Archie Brooks." She spoke rapidly and a shade too emphatically.

"His friends called him Chunky. He had a flat in Whitedown Gardens."

"What do you mean, he *had* a flat in Whitedown Gardens?"

Temple ignored Steve's pleading look. She had guessed what he was going to do.

"Brooks is dead. He was murdered."

Eileen's hand flew to her throat. "No . . . No! I don't believe it." Her cry echoed down the passage. "You're not serious . . ." she gasped, holding on to the door for support. "I don't believe it. You're lying! You're deliberately lying because you want to find out . . ."

Temple went past her to close the door. "I'm deliberately telling you the truth, Mrs Greene, because I want to find out how well you knew Archie Brooks!"

Eileen sat down on the nearest chair, a small Victorian nursing chair.

"When was he murdered?" she whispered.

Steve had moved to the window, turning her back as if to distance herself from the scene.

"Tuesday night. The evening before you telephoned him at his flat."

"It was you who answered!" Her eyes widened as she stared up at Temple. "That wasn't Chunky at all." Her voice hardened. "You tricked me, pretending to be him. Didn't you?"

"I can't claim credit for that. It was a man called James, Chief Inspector James."

"I told him about the meeting, didn't I? I told him that . . ." She stood up, suddenly tensing. "Were you at the flat when I telephoned?"

"Yes, I heard the whole conversation. It was me that suggested the impersonation."

"You might have spared me that! You might have had the decency to . . ." she twisted round to appeal to Steve, but Steve's back was still turned. "Who killed him? Who murdered Chunky?"

"I don't know, but with your help I'm going to find out. Why did you tell Brooks about the meeting?"

"I had to tell him because . . ."

"Because what?"

"I'm not going to say any more. I'm not talking." Eileen had regained control of herself. The set of her mouth was obstinate. "Please don't ask me any more questions."

But Temple wanted to follow up his advantage. "Now listen. How was Brooks mixed up in this business? Where was this meeting supposed to take place?"

"I don't know. Really, I don't know. Now please leave me alone. Don't ask me any more questions."

"Don't you see, I've got to ask you these questions? I've

got to know what's behind all this. Now tell me the truth, what did Chunky Brooks want you to find out?"

"I had to tell him – I made a promise that once I knew when . . . when . . . Oh, please leave me alone, Mr Temple." She reached for the back of the chair again and sat down, fighting back her sobs. "I can't talk now, I'm too upset. I was awfully fond of Chunky, he . . . "

"Paul, can't you see she's . . ." Steve intervened at last, unable to bear Eileen's distress any longer.

"Was Brooks a close friend?" Temple ignored his wife but his voice was more gentle.

"Yes, we'd known . . . each other ever since we were children." She choked on a sob. Temple handed her the clean handkerchief from his breast pocket. "He was always very kind to me."

"Eileen, I want you to have a look at this."

Temple dipped into the ticket pocket of his jacket and brought out the 1952 penny which Forbes had returned to him that morning.

"What is it?"

"It's a penny. My wife found it the night Archie was murdered. Have you ever seen a penny like this on a key-ring or a watch-chain or perhaps even on a bracelet?"

She dabbed her eyes with the handkerchief and tried to focus on the coin Temple was holding in front of her.

"No. No, I don't think so."

"Are you sure?"

"Yes, I'm quite sure."

Steve had come over to the side of Eileen's chair. She gave Temple a reproachful look.

"Are you feeling better now?"

"Yes, I'm all right," said Eileen softly.

"Don't you realise that I'm only trying to help you?" Temple was exasperated by the collusion of the two women. "Sooner or later, whether you like it or not, you're going to tell me all you know about this business. Why don't you tell me now?"

"Mr Temple, listen!" In one of her abrupt changes of mood Eileen was suddenly eager and friendly. "I'll tell you what I'll do. I'll come to your room tonight – late tonight when the others are in bed."

"But how can you?" said Steve "Won't your husband miss you?"

"No. We have separate rooms. My room's just along the corridor. I'll come tonight, Mr Temple. I promise you."

"Can I depend on that?" Temple asked dubiously.

"Yes. Yes, I promise!"

"All right."

Steve, nearest the door, had heard the creak of floor boards in the corridor. "I think there's someone coming, Paul!"

Eileen hastily stood up and inspected herself in the tilting cheval mirror. "Oh, dear! Oh, dear, I look dreadful!"

There came a single sharp knock on the door and at the same time it opened. Hubert Greene paused on the threshold, his alert eyes taking in the scene; Eileen with her eyes red and cheeks tear-stained, Steve's face still showing concern and Temple's features expressionless.

"What is it, Hubert?" Eileen asked with forced brightness.

"Lunch is ready, my dear," said Hubert, with a smile. He came into the room, took her hand and tenderly led her to the doorway. She went, as docile as a child. "Come down when you're ready," Hubert said over his shoulder to the Temples, and closed the door.

"Did you pack those socks, darling – the ones I bought in New York?"

"Yes, they're in the top drawer."

"Thanks. I enjoyed our walk this afternoon, Steve. It was a relief to have some time on our own."

After tea the Temples had escaped from the house party and at Eileen's suggestion had followed the path that circled the lake. It took them through the woods on the far side and back past the boat-house at the southern end of the half-mile stretch of water.

"Yes, so did I." Steve was inspecting herself in the cheval mirror. She had slipped into a plain chocolate velvet dress with long slim arms. It was hard to know what to wear in this house. Moira was quite capable of turning up to dinner in jeans. "Does this dress look all right?"

"Yes, of course it looks all right. It ought to, judging by what you paid for it."

"Now don't you start on that! Zip the back for me."

"What did Boyer have to say?" Temple asked, doing as he was told. "You seemed to be putting your heads together rather a lot."

"Oh, nothing. He told me he thought I'd make a very good dancer."

"By Timothy, the old technique! I wouldn't trust that tailor's dummy as far as I could throw him."

Steve inserted a stockinged foot into a shiny black court shoe. "Did you notice Moira Portland this morning when he said she was the world's worst nagger? She looked furious."

"Moira Portland's always looking furious. I'm inclined to agree with Greene about that young woman."

Steve sat down at the dressing table and started to brush her hair. "Paul, I don't know whether you've realised it or not, but George Kelly's avoiding us. He didn't even have tea with us this afternoon"

"He's probably frightened that one of us might mention that telephone call."

"Yes. Why do you think he made it, darling? He must have known that sooner or later we'd ask him about it."

"He obviously made it because . . ." Temple broke off at the sound of a knock on the door. "Come in."

Hubert Greene opened the door. He had changed into a dark suit and was wearing a bow tie.

"Excuse me . . ." He glanced apologetically at Steve, who did not turn round. "There's a telephone call for you, Temple."

"For me? Who is it, do you know?"

"I'm afraid I didn't ask. You can take it in my room if you like."

"Oh, thanks." Temple reached for his coat. "Shan't be a moment, darling."

Greene led him to a bedroom at the far end of the corridor. It was quite small and had the appearance of a bachelor's den. Temple wondered why the Greenes did not sleep together.

"Here we are. The 'phone's by the bed."

Temple saw that the receiver was already off its cradle. "Oh, thanks."

"Can you find your way back all right?"

"Yes, rather."

"When you and Mrs Temple are ready we're having drinks in the drawing-room."

"Fine."

Greene went out and tactfully closed the door.

Temple took his time about sitting on the bed and picking up the receiver.

"Hello?"

"Hello, is that you, Temple?"

"Oh, hello, Sir Graham!"

"Sorry if I've interrupted your dinner."

"No, as a matter of fact we were just going down."

"You did say give me a ring, remember?"

"Yes, of course."

"I think we're making headway, Temple – at last."

"Oh, good. I thought you sounded optimistic. What's happened?"

"Are you alone?"

"Yes."

Temple was being watched, but only by the faces in the photographs. There was one on the chest of drawers of Eileen in a swim suit beside a blue pool.

"Is it all right – to talk, I mean?"

"Yes, I think so."

"Well, Temple, listen. We've discovered the identity of Dr Elzec and we know at least one of his contacts. We came across his photograph in a snapshot album – the one you and James found at Archie Brooks'."

"Oh, I see."

"His real name is Wilderhof. He was mixed up in the Basle counterfeit racket in 1984."

"Are you sure of that?"

"I'm quite sure."

"What are you going to do about it, Sir Graham?"

"There's no point in picking him up. In any case, we've nothing on him at the moment. You can't arrest a man for paying five hundred pounds a week for a furnished flat."

"Are you watching him?"

"Yes, there's a man on the block night and day. You'll probably spot him when you get back on Monday morning."

"You seem to have been pretty busy since I left town, Sir Graham."

"Yes. Get in touch with me as soon as you get back, Temple."

"I'll do that."

Forbes had hung up. Temple went on listening for a few seconds before he quietly replaced his own instrument.

Back in the guest bedroom he found Steve dressed and ready, ear-rings and a necklace in place and a silk shawl over her arm in case it grew chillier.

"Oh, I was just going to go down, darling. Are you ready?"

"I'll be ready when I put a tie on."

"Who was it on the 'phone?"

"Sir Graham."

"Oh, did he want anything special?"

"No, he—" Temple chuckled as he knotted his tie, "just wanted a chat."

"What's the joke?"

"I've got a hunch we shall find somebody rather on edge this evening, Steve. It'll be interesting to see who it is."

"Why do you say that?"

"Before I left town I made arrangements for Sir Graham to 'phone and pretend that the Yard had discovered the real identity of Dr Elzec. I also told him to tell me that they'd discovered who his contact was."

"But what was the point of that? Why should he say those things if they weren't true?"

Temple was brushing the shoulders and lapels of his jacket. "I was pretty certain that any telephone conversation I had would be listened to."

"Do you think someone did listen to your conversation?"

"Yes, I'm sure of it."

"Paul, you looked puzzled just now. Did Sir Graham say anything else?"

"I'm surprised he told me that the Yard know Elzec's real name is Wilderhof and that he was mixed up in the Basle currency racket in 1984. He probably knew as well as I did that the conversation was being listened to."

"He probably wants to use Elzec or Wilderhof or whatever his name is as a bait. If the people behind this affair think that Elzec's been found out they'll probably try to get rid of him."

"Yes."

"And that's when Sir Graham'll step in."

"There might be something in that, Steve." Temple agreed rather absent-mindedly. "I shouldn't be surprised. Come along, darling, let's go down."

All but one of the house party had assembled in the drawing room when the Temples joined them. Hubert and Eileen Greene, Stella Portland, Chris Boyer and George Kelly had all changed into something different, though no one could be said to be in formal evening dress. The french windows had been closed and Hubert Greene was again busy at the drinks cabinet seeing that everyone had the drink they wanted.

"Oh, dear, are we the last?" Steve apologised.

"You're not," said Eileen. "Moira has not appeared yet."

While Hubert was pouring a dry Martini and a fino sherry for Temple and Steve the other two ladies were admiring the latter's dress. Temple tried to engage Boyer in conversation but he was clearly concerned by the non-appearance of his fiancée.

It was a good five minutes before she came in. She was wearing a short black dress with a diamond clip on each shoulder.

"Come in, Moira," Hubert greeted her, pleasantly enough. "We've been waiting for you."

Chris Boyer was less relaxed. "Where on earth have you been, Moira? You were ready ages ago."

"I've been for a walk," she declared defiantly. "Is there any particular reason why I shouldn't go for a walk before dinner?"

"No, of course not."

"Say, you look all steamed up about something," said George Kelly with his usual lack of tact. "You need a drink."

"Excellent advice, Mr Kelly – if a slight understatement." Moira was flushed, the pupils of her eyes seemed larger and her hands were clenching. "I need several drinks."

"What would you like, Moira?" Hubert spoke quietly, but he was studying her carefully.

"It's all right, I'll mix it."

"I'm mixing the drinks, Moira." Hubert interrupted her firmly. "What would you like?"

"I'll have a Bloody Mary."

"Have you been drinking already?" Boyer said quickly.

"What do you mean – already?" She swung round to face him, pouting. "I've had three very small pink gins, if that's what you mean."

Stella gave a slightly forced laugh. "Where on earth did you have those?"

"I drove down into the village."

"I thought you said you'd been for a walk?" Hubert pointed out. Moira had chosen a drink that needed a lot of preparation. He had poured the vodka and tomato juice and was hunting for the Worcester sauce and the tabasco.

"I drove down into the village, I got out of my car and I walked – on my own two legs – into a very large pub and ordered three very small pink gins." Moira was becoming at the same time more defiant and more illogical as she faced each of her interlocutors in turn. "Is there anything else you'd like to know?"

"Yes," said Temple crisply.

"What?" Moira spun round to face this new threat.

"Where's my sherry?"

"Oh, I'm sorry, Temple," Hubert apologised. "I poured it out and left it on the trolley. Here we are."

As Hubert handed Temple his glass Moira demanded, "And what about my Bloody Mary, Hubert?"

"Look here, Moira." said Boyer, distressed and concerned, "I think you've had far too much already."

"Darling, I'm not interested in what you think. As a matter of fact, sweetie, I'm not at all sure that you *can* think." Moira was speaking with a brittle, bright-eyed clarity, staring her fiancé in the face. "You're a tall, upright, well creased slice of sartorial perfection, but when it comes to brains . . . "

"Miss Portland, please." Even the quiet Eileen was moved to protest.

"No. No, please. I'm finding this very interesting," said Boyer, his eyes hard. "This is a new side to my fiancée. It seems to me that I ought to get acquainted with it."

"Careful, Chris. Careful." Moira mocked him. "Those are mighty big words." She turned on Hubert. "Where's my drink?"

"Here we are." Hubert handed her the half-pint glass.

"Miss Portland, you really oughtn't to have another drink before dinner," Eileen protested.

"Do you agree, Mr Temple? Do you think I oughtn't to have another drink?"

"You're over twenty-one, Miss Portland," said Temple equably. "You know what you're doing."

"You'll finish up with a duodenal, baby." Kelly told her. "That's what you'll finish up with."

"Why, Mr Kelly. I didn't know you cared! Skoal everybody!" Moira tilted her head back and downed the drink in one long draught. She gasped, staring into the empty glass. "Don't look so worried, Eileen, I can take it."

"Boy," Kelly breathed in admiration, "you certainly can take it!"

Stella had been watching this distressing exhibition with more compassion than the others. Now she stepped in. "I think you'd better go to your room, Moira."

"I'll do nothing of the sort. Why should I go to my room? I'm not a school-girl. I'm not going to anybody's room. I'm going to have another drink."

"Come along, Moira. I'll take you up to your room." Boyer took hold of her arm. She flung him off angrily.

"Don't touch me! Don't put your hands on me! Do you hear what I say, leave me alone!"

Abruptly her face crumpled. She swayed and her eyes rolled upwards. To his credit Boyer put a hand out to steady her.

"Whatever is the matter with the girl?" Stella remarked, her disgust written on her face.

"You know what's the matter," Moira shouted, galvanised by the comment. "You know what's the matter with me all right. One of you in this room murdered Chunky! I only found that out tonight! He was the only friend I had. He understood me. There was no nonsense with Chunky." The last part of her appalling declaration was drowned by her sobs. "He was a real friend."

"Come along, Moira," said Eileen quietly. "Let me take you to your room."

In a way the drink had helped. Moira had given vent to the agony she was feeling. Leaning on Eileen, she allowed herself to be led away.

It was Stella who broke the embarrassed silence. "Well!

You said she was a temperamental young woman but I certainly never thought she was that bad."

"Oh, that's nothing," Hubert assured her. "Sometimes she gets completely out of hand. I really wonder what the devil we're going to do with her."

"Who's this guy Chunky she was on about?" Kelly demanded.

"Chunky was a man called Archie Brooks," said Temple. "He was attached to Scotland Yard."

"Was he murdered – or was she just making that up?"

"He was murdered, Mr Kelly. Three or four nights ago. As a matter of fact he was murdered outside the Manila, the night you telephoned my wife."

"But why should I telephone Mrs Temple?" Kelly objected with a puzzled frown.

"Don't you remember what you said to me that night?" Steve asked him.

"Well, if I don't remember speaking to you I'm hardly likely to recall what I said."

"You warned me to advise my husband to keep out of the Madison case," Steve told him tersely.

"What's the Madison case?"

"Sam Portland had an appointment to see a private detective called Madison. Unfortunately he died of heart failure and was unable to keep the appointment." Steve glanced at Paul, but he was listening without expression to the verbal duel. "I've got a hunch that if Portland had kept that appointment he'd have discovered that Madison was no more a private detective than you are. If you want my frank opinion . . . "

"Sure," said Kelly, leading her on with a mocking smile. "Let's have your frank opinion, Mrs Temple."

"If you want my frank opinion I think Madison's a blackmailer and the leader of a racket for distributing counterfeit dollars."

"You know, you've got some queer notions inside that pretty head of yours. What else am I supposed to have told you over the telephone?"

"You said, 'Tell your husband to keep out of the Madison case. If he doesn't he's going to get mixed up with a bunch of very unpleasant customers.'"

Kelly pretended to be shocked at the suggestion. "Did I say that?"

"You did, Mr Kelly." Steve was angry now as she faced Kelly. "You also said that *you* were one of the unpleasant customers."

"Why, that's a dreadful thing to say to anybody, it's almost a threat." Kelly appealed to the small audience who had been following the exchange. "You don't think I'm an unpleasant customer, do you, Mr Temple?"

"I think you are a very slippery one, Mr Kelly," said Temple frankly.

"What the hell does it matter whether he 'phoned your wife or not?" Boyer interrupted the dialogue angrily. "Didn't you hear what Moira said? She said that someone in this room – one of us – murdered Archie Brooks. Now, who was she getting at?"

"Don't look at me, brother!" Kelly shrank away in mock apprehension. "I'd never even heard of Brooks until that crazy dame of yours mentioned him."

"Did you know Archie Brooks, Mr Boyer?" Steve asked shrewdly.

"Yes, I did. I knew him, I liked him and I didn't murder him."

"Well, that seems conclusive enough." Stella turned to her host. "What about you, Hubert?"

"I'd never heard of the fellow until Moira mentioned him." Hubert glanced round with relief as Eileen came back into the room. "How is she?"

"She's all right now. I've given her a sedative and she's lying down. Shall we go into dinner, Hubert?"

The grandfather clock in the hall had chimed three quarters and then struck three reverberating notes.

"Paul, are you awake?"

"Yes."

"It's three o'clock."

"Yes, I know."

Steve had put a dressing-gown on over her nightdress and got into bed. For the last two hours she had been trying to keep herself awake by reading that month's number of *Harper's and Queen*. Paul had discarded his jacket in favour of a cardigan and settled down in a wing-backed Victorian chair to read the latest Noel Barber novel, which he had found in the guest bedroom book-case.

"It doesn't look as if she's coming, does it?"

"Well, she promised to come, didn't she? I hope she does because I've got a feeling that Mrs Greene knows quite a lot about this affair."

"Yes." Temple laid the book down on the arm-rest. "You know, Steve, there's one rather interesting point about all this. I don't know whether you've spotted it or not."

"Yes, I've spotted it, darling. So far we haven't heard from Mr Madison."

"So far."

"Did you hear them come up to bed?"

"I heard Greene. I don't know whether Eileen was with him or not. It must have been about half past twelve."

Temple got up from the chair and stretched. "Steve, where's my cigarette lighter?"

"It's on the dressing table." Steve swung her legs out of bed and put her bedroom slippers on.

"Do you want a cigarette, darling?"

"No, thanks."

"I'm going to give her another half an hour." Temple held the flame to his cigarette. "If she's not here by half past three I'm . . . "

"What is it?"

Temple had cocked his head, listening. For hours now the big house had been silent, bar the occasional creak of a floor board settling.

"I thought I heard something."

"Probably a bird down by the lake, they don't seem to need any sleep."

"No. This was in the house. Sh! Listen!"

They both strained their ears, listening. This time the creak of a floor board sounded nearer. Then came a faint, almost shy tap on the door.

"There's someone at the door, Paul!"

"Good. I thought she'd come."

Before he had time to stub his cigarette out the faint tap was repeated. Temple crossed to the door and opened it.

"Why, Mr Greene!" he exclaimed. Hubert was standing there, wild-eyed and distraught.

"What is it?"

"I'm awfully sorry to disturb you, Temple – but have you seen my wife?"

"Your wife?"

"Yes." Hubert came into the room and closed the door. Temple saw that his hands were shaking.

"No, I'm afraid we haven't."

"Isn't she in bed?" Steve suggested.

"No, I went along to her room about a quarter of an hour ago. Eileen wasn't there and the bed hadn't been slept in."

"She's probably in the bathroom."

"No, Mrs Temple. I've looked in the bathroom."

"Well, perhaps she's with Mrs Portland or . . . "

"No, she's not with Mrs Portland or Moira." Hubert's face was bleak and strained. If Temple had been in his own house he would have prescribed a stiff whisky. "As a matter of fact I've been all over the house and there just isn't a sign of her."

"Have you spoken to your staff?"

"Yes, I've just come from their quarters."

"Well – what time did she go to bed?"

"She went to bed when I did just after twelve. You must have heard us, Temple, your light was still on. It's most uncanny, I just don't—"

Hubert's nerves were on edge. He started violently as there came a loud thud on the door. It was far too violent to be a knock. "Good God! What's that, Temple?"

Steve too had been shocked by the brutal sound in the silence of the night. "Paul, what on earth was that?"

It took Temple only a few seconds to stride across the room and open the door. He stared out into the dark corridor. Then, as the door swung open wider, the light from inside the room showed a large knife embedded in the wood.

"It's a knife! Someone must have thrown it at the door."

"Did you see anybody?" Hubert asked in a shaky voice.

"No, there's no one in the corridor."

"Paul . . . There's a note! Look! It's on the knife."

Temple swung the door right back. Now he could see the slip of paper impaled on the knife, just where the blade met the handle. It required quite an effort to pull the knife free. Carefully he slid the folded note up the blade and opened it out.

91

"What does it say?"

Temple handed the paper to Steve. She stared at it. "It says – 'Go to the boat-house' . . . "

"The boat-house?" Hubert echoed. "Is that all it says?"

"Yes."

"That must be the boat-house on the far side of the lake, Steve. We passed it this afternoon. Greene," Temple turned urgently to his host, "can you find a torch somewhere? I'll meet you downstairs."

"Temple, you don't think . . . "

"Do as I say! I'll meet you downstairs in three minutes!"

When Temple went down Greene was already waiting in the hall. He had put on an anorak over the suit he had been wearing at dinner and armed himself with a substantial torch. Temple had donned a pair of strong walking shoes and an overcoat. He had instructed Steve to lock the door of her room and open to nobody until he returned.

Greene was pale and apprehensive as he opened the front door. The moon was only half full and kept dodging behind clouds.

"Don't use your torch, Greene. We don't want to advertise our presence. Someone may be waiting down at the boat-house."

Once they were clear of the house their eyes adjusted to the darkness. Temple could see the outline of the trees and the paler shape of the avenue snaking down the hill and around the lake. Its waters gleamed dully in the moonlight. In the gloom it was easier to believe the superstition that it was bottomless.

Greene led the way down a footpath that cut across the loop in the avenue. Temple looked back once at the house. Only one light showed, in the window of the room where he had left Steve.

Suddenly he wanted to be finished with this as quickly as possible, so that he could get back to her. The knife-borne message could have been no more than a ruse to lure him out of the house.

"You lead the way," Temple said when they reached the path leading through the wood to the boat-house. "I'll cover your back."

He did not relish the thought of leaving his own back exposed to anyone so unpredictable as Hubert Greene.

They were threading the same path as he had walked that afternoon with Steve, but in the opposite direction. Here among the trees it was very much darker.

Greene stumbled over an exposed root and nervously flashed his torch on the ground.

"Put it out!" commanded Temple.

The boat-house loomed up suddenly, its gabled outline silhouetted against the faintly luminous lake. Greene stopped.

"What do we do now?" he whispered.

"We'll have a look in the boat-house, there's a boat in it, isn't there?"

"Should be," muttered Greene. "We use the upper part for storing."

With Temple behind him, he went to the door and opened it. In the dark interior a rowing boat could just be seen, shifting restlessly on the moving water. The only sound was the gentle slapping of waves on its stern.

"All right to use the torch now?" Greene asked, still whispering.

Temple closed the door behind him. "Yes, it's O.K. now."

Greene switched his torch on. He directed the beam round the wooden walls of the boat-house, into the boat itself.

"There's no one here. But the oars are wet. Someone's been using the boat recently."

Temple still had his back against the door. He was listening to Greene but he was also listening for any other sound. His eyes had now adjusted to the more intense darkness inside the boat-house. He had avoided looking directly at Greene's torch.

Something seemed to be glowing in the water close to his feet, just under the bow of the boat, something lighter than the weeds that waved in the black water.

"Shine your torch here, Greene. Under the bow of the boat."

Greene came back to where Temple was standing. He directed the beam into the water.

"My God!" He went down on one knee to look more closely. He gasped and turned his head to look up. The light of the torch reflected by the water cast a weird shadow across his face. "It's a hand, Temple. Somebody's hand!"

5   Concerning Steve

Temple untied the painter by which the boat was moored to a bollard on the wooden platform that ran round the sides of the boat-house. He pushed the boat out till it was at the full length of the rope.

Greene shone his torch into the water again. "There *is* someone in the water."

Temple took off his shoes. Facing the wooden platform he lowered himself into the water, testing its depth. When it was at waist level, he touched bottom, a soft slithery bottom.

"Give me your hand, Greene. I'm going to see if I can reach it."

The movement of the boat had disturbed the body which had wafted further away, as if reluctant to keep this rendezvous. With Greene's hand to steady him and his torch stabbing through the water Temple managed to locate and seize the ephemeral hand.

As he pulled, the body came to him quite willingly, made weightless by the water. It was face downwards.

"It's a woman." Temple had seen that long, dark hair. "Help me. We've got to get her out."

Greene put down his torch. Its beam shone out across the lake. With Temple in the water and Greene hauling from the platform, they managed to heave the suddenly heavy body out and lay it face upwards on the platform.

Temple hauled himself clear of the ice-cold water. Greene retrieved his torch and shone it on the face.

"Temple! It's Eileen!" He almost dropped the torch. Temple grabbed it from him. "Do you hear me? It's my wife!"

Hubert had gone down on his knees, trying to lift and hold the lifeless form of his wife, still in the dress she had worn for dinner.

"Help me, Temple! I've got to give her the kiss of life, artificial respiration, something."

Temple had focussed the torch on the pathetic tableau,

the anguished husband clasping his wife, her head lolling in the crook of his elbow.

"It's no good, Greene. I'm sorry. Look at your hands."

"What?"

"Look at your hands."

Greene kept a hold with one hand and stared at the other.

"It's blood!" he choked. "She's been stabbed!"

He let the body go. It dropped to the boards, the head striking them with a thud. A dreadful retching sound filled the boat-house. It was Greene, vomiting uncontrollably.

As Temple passed through the hall, the hands of the old grandfather clock were pointing to seven minutes past midday. Nine hours had passed since Hubert Greene had knocked on the guest-room door and Temple had not been to bed during that time. Indeed there had been little sleep for anyone in the house that night. The Surrey CID had arrived within an hour of Temple's 'phone call and the gravel circle in front of the house was soon filled with the cars of the Scene of Crime Officer, the CID Inspector, the doctor, pathologist and forensic scientist and half a dozen photographers, finger-print experts and plain-clothes detectives. The immediate area of the boat-house had been roped off and was now being subjected to a minute examination. Sir Graham had arrived with Chief Inspector James just as a very subdued house-party were finishing breakfast. The obvious link with the murder of Archie Brooks meant that they would work in close co-operation with the Surrey CID.

Temple could hear the sound of voices as he approached the drawing-room door. The conversation ceased abruptly as he entered the room. Stella Portland was sitting on the sofa. She was obviously still suffering from the shock of the news with which she had been awakened at four a.m. There were shadows under her eyes and she had made no attempt to do her face up. Chris Boyer was at the french windows, staring moodily out over the terrace. George Kelly appeared to be his usual cocky self. He had been helping himself to whisky from the drinks cabinet.

"Is Miss Portland here?"

"No, she's in her room," Stella replied. "Do you want her?"

"Sir Graham would like to have a word with her. He's in the library."

"I'll tell her," Boyer offered, moving away from the window.

"No, that's all right, Boyer," Temple said firmly. "Would you mind fetching her, Mrs Portland?"

"No, of course not." Stella rose and went out of the room, closing the door behind her.

"Temple, I'm not trying to be difficult," Kelly complained, "but when's Sir Graham going to let us go? He does nothing but ask us the same questions over and over again."

"You seem to forget, Mr Kelly, a murder has been committed."

"I know a murder's been committed. We're not likely to forget it, any of us. Look, Temple, let's put our cards on the table. I know why the Yard have got their eye on me. Mrs Greene was stabbed, wasn't she?"

"Yes. And so was Archie Brooks."

"I didn't know that."

"I may be dense, Temple," Boyer cut in, "but I don't see the significance."

"I used to do a knife-throwing act," Kelly told him with a grin. "They still think I'm doing it. Catch on?"

"But that's nonsense!" exclaimed Boyer. "Why on earth should you want to murder Eileen?"

Temple produced the knife he had been holding behind his back. "Kelly, does this knife belong to you?"

"Why, yes. I've got several knives like that. I told you, I used to do a circus act."

"But you don't still do it?"

"Only as a gag. I take the knives with me when I'm invited anywhere." Kelly saw the expression on Temple's face. "Well — you know how it is — some people like to do conjuring tricks, others do card tricks . . . "

"And you throw knives?" Temple was holding the knife by the tip of the blade, as if he was contemplating throwing it at Kelly. "Did you throw this last night?"

"Good Lord!" Boyer had been staring at the knife in fascination. "You don't mean this is the knife that killed Eileen Greene?"

"No, Boyer. This knife was thrown at my bedroom door just after three o'clock this morning. There was a note attached to it which said 'Go down to the boat-house'. Greene and I went down – and found Eileen."

Boyer stared at Kelly with a new expression on his face. From now on he was less inclined to ridicule Temple's suggestion. Temple turned to Kelly again.

"So you see, Kelly, I'm not accusing you of murder." Temple lowered the knife. "I'm simply asking you . . . "

"If I got up at three o'clock in the morning and threw a knife at your bedroom door?"

"Exactly."

"The answer's no."

"Then somebody must have stolen the knife from you?"

"That seems to be the obvious explanation."

"How many knives have you?"

"I arrived at Southampton with four."

"That's not what I asked you. How many knives have you now?"

"There should be three in my room – the one you've got there makes four."

"How do you know you've still got three?"

Unsettled by Temple's quick-fire questions Kelly stared at his glass. He was regretting the two double whiskies he had swallowed.

"Because I was looking at them this morning and . . . "

"You were? Then you must have noticed that this one was missing?"

"Yes, I did—" Kelly began, then added lamely. "I thought I'd left it in town."

Stella, entering the room at that moment, stopped on the threshold. She had picked up the tension between the two men facing each other.

"Moira will be down in a few moments."

"Oh, thank you, Mrs Portland."

Stella came forward nervously into the room. She glanced at George, who was trying to convey a silent message to her.

"Mr Kelly and I would like to catch the two forty-five back to town. Is that possible?"

"I don't see why not," said Temple pleasantly. "I'll have a word with Sir Graham."

"Thank you. And, Mr Temple . . . Do you know where Hubert is? We haven't seen him since breakfast."

"He's in his room."

"How's he taking all this?"

"Well, naturally, he's very distressed."

"Yes, of course." Stella's eyes toured the room, as if visualising Eileen welcoming her guests on the previous morning. "What a dreadful thing to have happened – really dreadful. Have you any idea who did it?"

"Yes, Mrs Portland, I have." Temple moved to the door. "I'll ask Sir Graham about the train."

As he went out he could feel three pairs of eyes boring into his back and not one of them was friendly.

Moira had still not come down when Temple rejoined Forbes and James in the library. James had taken over the long table in the middle of the room. It was already littered with statements. Forbes, his usual restless self, was prowling the room, pausing from time to time to peruse the titles of the rows and rows of leather-bound classics. Lord Dalesdon had obviously been something of a scholar. The bright sunshine sparkling on the flowers and shrubs outside the window was in sharp contrast to the gloomy atmosphere inside the house.

James had his back to the door and was arguing his point of view as Temple entered the room.

"The whole point, Sir Graham, is – if she was murdered in the house and carried down to the boat-house we would expect there to be blood-stains and a trail . . . "

He broke off as he realised Temple had returned.

"Am I interrupting?"

"No, of course not, Temple," Forbes assured him. "We were just discussing whether this murder really has anything to do with the Archie Brooks business."

"I think it's all part and parcel of the same case, Sir Graham."

"Then why was she murdered? We've got a pretty good notion why Brooks was taken care of, but this affair isn't quite the same."

"If Temple's right, Sir Graham – and I must confess, I'm inclined to agree with him – then it seems to me that this Madison . . . " James broke off at the sound of the door closing. Moira had come into the room without knocking.

She was wearing the same denim skirt and her manner was as defiant as ever.

"You wanted to see me?"

"Oh yes, come in, Miss Portland." Forbes was courteous, as he always was with women. "Won't you sit down?"

"I should prefer to stand, if you don't mind."

"Just as you wish." Forbes went to sit in the chair beside James. He picked up half a dozen sheets of A4 paper clipped together. "I've been reading through your statement, Miss Portland. There are one or two points I'm not quite clear about."

"Well?" Moira had clasped her hands behind her back. Temple could see that her fingers were clenching and unclenching.

"You say you went to your room last night at about a quarter past eight – before dinner – you took a sedative and went to bed."

"Yes."

"I understand from Mr Temple that earlier in the evening you caused rather an unpleasant scene."

"Yes, I was tight." She said it in a voice that expressed no compunction. "I'm afraid I behaved very badly."

"Well, you made rather a remarkable statement."

"Did I? I'm afraid I don't remember."

"You said that Archie Brooks was a friend of yours and that he'd been murdered by 'someone in this room.'" Forbes lifted his eyes from the paper and levelled them at her. "It was obvious that you were referring to one of five people – Mr and Mrs Greene, Mr Kelly, Mrs Portland, or your fiancé, Mr Boyer."

"I've told you I don't remember making such a statement."

"Nevertheless, you made it."

"I was drunk. I just didn't know what I was saying."

"Was Archie Brooks a friend of yours?"

Moira's eyes had shifted to James. He was ostentatiously noting down her answers.

"Yes."

"A close friend?"

"It depends what you mean by a close friend." She managed to imply that Forbes would know what a close friend meant.

"Well, did you see a great deal of each other?" persisted Forbes patiently.

"No, he came to the Manila once or twice and . . . " she shrugged, "we had a few drinks together. That's all."

"You seem to be fond of having a few drinks."

Moira's resentment was beginning to show. She half turned as if to walk out. "Is there anything else you'd like to know?"

"Yes, there is." Forbes took an object from a white plastic bag lying on the table. "Have you seen this knife before?"

Moira barely glanced at the murder weapon. "No."

"Are you sure?"

"Quite sure."

Forbes put the knife back in the bag. He glanced inquiringly at James. James shook his head, implying that he had no questions. Forbes continued his interrogation. "When did you first hear that Mrs Greene had been murdered?"

"My fiancé told me. He came to my room."

"What time would that be?"

"About half past four."

"Were you surprised?"

"Of course I was surprised!" Moira turned her head towards Temple, who had walked into her field of vision. "I was stunned. I just didn't believe it."

"Is this the first time you've been down here – to 'Brown Acres'?"

"No. I've been down several times."

"Mm. I understand you work for Mr Greene?"

"I'm attached to the London office of the Portland Yeast Company, if that's what you mean."

"Mr Greene's office?"

A faintly disdainful smile tugged at Moira's lips. "Mr Greene is in charge of the office, yes."

Forbes had temporarily run out of questions and James did not seem inclined to take over from his superior. Temple took the opportunity to put his question.

"Miss Portland, when I met your father on the boat, coming over from America, he told me that Mr Greene had made arrangements for him to meet a man called Madison. Have you heard of Mr Madison by any chance?"

Moira had turned to face him. "No, I'm afraid I haven't."

"I see. Mr Greene doesn't seem to have heard of Madison either. It's most odd."

"You must have misunderstood my father," she said, her tone less hostile than when she had been answering Forbes.

"No, I don't think I did."

"Well, I'm sorry I can't help you." She switched back to Sir Graham. "May I go now?"

"Yes, you can go."

"Oh, just a moment." Moira was heading for the door when James' voice stopped her. "You said last night you'd been down to the village, to the local pub."

"Yes."

"Which one did you go to?"

"There's only one. The White Horse."

Temple murmured, "The White Swan."

"I mean The White Swan," Moira corrected herself angrily.

"If I remember rightly, you had three pink gins." James had been consulting his notes. "Is that right?"

"Yes."

"How do you account for the fact that no one seems to remember serving you, Miss Portland?" Moira did not answer. "Now, I ask you. A very pretty, well-dressed girl strolls into a quiet bar and orders three pink gins and yet no one seems to remember. Most odd."

"I can't see why," said Moira, but her defiance was crumbling.

Temple asked her quietly, "Did you really go down to the village last night?"

"Of course I did! How else did I manage to get drunk so quickly?"

"I don't think you were drunk, Miss Portland."

Moira was startled by Temple's remark, but she managed to greet it with a look of ridicule.

"Sir Graham, I'm going back to town this afternoon – have you any objection?"

"None whatever." He looked at James. "We've got her address, I take it?"

"Yes sir, we've got her address."

Moira turned at the door. "If you want to get in touch with me during the week you can find me at the office."

"Thank you," said Forbes, still polite.

The door closed on Moira. Immediately the tension level in the library dropped. James leant back, stretched his arms and exhaled a long breath. "That was a bit like interrogating a spitting cobra. What did you mean, Temple, you don't think she was drunk?"

Forbes forestalled Temple's answer to James' question.

"Temple, you don't think she overheard our telephone conversation, got scared and had to pretend she was tight to conceal her feelings?"

"It's a possibility, Sir Graham," Temple said non-commitally. Then changing the subject, "I've been meaning to ask you about that 'phone call. Was that a lot of nonsense about Dr Elzec or did you really come across his photograph?"

"Oh, we came across it all right. It was in the snapshot album you found at Brooks' place. Elzec, or Wilderhof as he called himself in '84, seems to be quite a character. He's been mixed up in all sorts of rackets."

"Is he a doctor?"

"Not a medical doctor. He's a doctor of music."

"Oh, I see. Why did you tell me about him over the 'phone – wasn't that risky?"

"I wanted whoever was listening to know that we were on to him. I believe that if Elzec really is mixed up in this business they'll either go for him or drop him like a hot potato. Don't worry, we've got our eye on Dr Elzec. With a bit of luck he might turn out to be a first-class decoy."

"I hope you're right, Sir Graham. I sincerely hope you're right."

Steve and Temple were back in Eaton Square by late afternoon. Steve carried her beauty case and a small flight bag into the hall, leaving Temple to take their two suitcases from the boot. The lift was at the second floor. She pressed the button to bring it down and watched the panel of numbers. The lift had reached the ground floor and the automatic doors had opened by the time Temple came into the hall. He put the two suitcases into the lift and Steve followed with her beauty case and flight bag. She was just about to press the touch button for the third floor when the hall doors were pushed open.

"Hold it, Steve."

The tall blond man who had come in quickened his step

when he saw that the lift was about to ascend.

Temple put out an arm to prevent the door closing.

"Good evening, Dr Elzec. You're going up?"

"Oh, good evening, Mr Temple. There is room for one more?"

"It's a bit of a crush with all our luggage but—"

Elzec was tall but not stout. He was mackintoshed and bare-headed and was carrying a black Samsonite brief-case.

"I don't think you've met my wife."

While Steve and Elzec exchanged civilities Temple pressed the touch button. The lift began to ascend.

"Have you been away for the weekend?" Elzec inquired conversationally.

"Yes, we've only just got back."

"I'm rather glad I bumped into you, Mr Temple, there's something I wanted to speak to you about. You'll probably think it's a lot of nonsense, but . . . "

"No, no, go on, Doctor."

"Mr Temple, if I wanted to speak to someone at Scotland Yard, do you think you could arrange it for me?"

"May I ask why?"

"Well, the fact of the matter is, Mr Temple," said Elzec, looking embarrassed, "I think I'm being followed."

"Being followed?" Temple repeated with incredulity.

"Yes. The first time I noticed it was yesterday morning. I had an appointment in Regent Street and I picked up a taxi just outside the flat. When I was getting into the taxi I noticed a man standing in one of the doorways."

"Yes?" prompted Temple, his tone still sceptical.

"Later, the same morning, when I was walking down Oxford Street, I noticed the same man. He was on the opposite side of the road but I'm sure he was watching me."

Temple smiled reassuringly. "It doesn't necessarily mean you're being followed just because you see the same man twice in one day."

"But I saw him again this afternoon. I had an appointment in Knightsbridge. I caught the tube from Green Park. When I got into the train he was already there, sitting in the corner, watching me . . . "

"Did you speak to him?"

"No, of course not."

"Have you any idea who he is – or why he's following you?"

Elzec gave a shrug. "No, not the slightest."

The lift had bumped to a stop at the third floor. As the door opened Elzec stepped out to allow a clear passage for the Temples to extract their luggage.

"All right, I'll have a word with the Yard about it," said Temple. "If you see him again or anything else develops give me a ring."

"Thank you, Mr Temple. That's very kind of you."

Elzec got back into the lift just in time to stop the doors closing on him. He was still clutching his brief-case. He touched the button and turned to give the Temples a good-neighbourly smile.

Temple had just finished his unpacking when he heard the door bell ring – or rather it would be true to say that he had turned his suitcase upside down and emptied the contents onto the bed. There was only one thing he hated more than packing and that was unpacking. Glad of the excuse to leave Steve to sort his things out and put them away neatly in drawers and wardrobe, he went through the hall to open the door. Monday was Charlie's evening off, or one of them.

Temple already had a shrewd idea who his caller was and it was no great surprise to see Sir Graham on the doormat. He seemed very pleased with himself as he hung his coat and hat up and followed Temple into the drawing-room.

His first question, when he saw that there was no one else in the room, was, "Is Steve in?"

"Yes, she's unpacking, she'll be here in a minute. Now, what can I get you to drink, Sir Graham?"

"Nothing, thanks."

"Sure?"

"Quite sure, thanks."

Forbes was fidgety. Temple knew he had a great admiration for Steve, but he had never made it quite so obvious that she was the person he had really called to see.

"I'm glad you called round, Sir Graham. I just bumped into Elzec."

"Oh, when?" asked Forbes, without any great interest.

"About twenty minutes ago. He asked me to have a word

with you. He's under the impression that he's being followed."

"Oh, Lord! You mean . . . "

"Yes, he's spotted your man. I'm afraid you'll have to change him, put someone a little more discreet on the job."

"That's annoying. Oh well, I'll have a word with James."

"Hello, Sir Graham."

Forbes visibly brightened as Steve came into the room. "Oh, hello, Steve."

"You look rather pleased with yourself. What's happened?"

"We've had the break we've been waiting for, Steve. When I got back to the Yard I found that a message had come in from Interpol."

"Yes?"

"It informs us that a man called Dordrecht has booked a flight from Amsterdam to London tomorrow afternoon."

"Dordrecht?"

Temple was wondering why Forbes had reserved this information until Steve had appeared. "I haven't heard that name before."

"Paul, haven't you offered Sir Graham a drink?" said Steve reproachfully.

"I'm not drinking, Steve, thank you. I can't really stay. Dordrecht operates under several names, Temple. He's ostensibly an import-export merchant and lives just outside Amsterdam, near the airport. The Dutch police are sure that one of his imports is counterfeit dollars. They've been watching him for months, waiting for an opportunity to drop on him."

Whilst talking, Forbes had gravitated by force of habit to the chair he always occupied when he was in this room. Steve gratefully followed his example and sat down on the sofa.

"Our Dutch colleagues are confident that he's coming over here to contact his head man – call him Madison, if you like – and collect a consignment of dollars. He's only booked one way and the Dutch are curious to know not only who he contacts but how he plans to return home with his counterfeit dollars."

"What are you going to do – tail him at this end?"

"Of course. From the moment he steps off the plane we'll

watch him like hawks. In my opinion there's a very good chance that he might lead us straight to Madison."

"Yes, and there's also a very good chance he might vanish into thin air."

"Yes, I've thought of that, Temple." Forbes glanced uneasily at Steve. "As a matter of fact, that's why I'm here."

"Oh, you want me to pop over to Amsterdam and fly back on the same 'plane?"

"No, I don't want you to pop anywhere, Temple."

"Why not?"

"Dordrecht is a man for the ladies," Forbes explained, uncharacteristically apologetic. "He has a wife and family in Holland, but when he travels abroad he likes to have his little fling. He's a very presentable chap and speaks excellent English and he fancies rather high-class goods."

Steve had been watching Forbes' embarrassment with amusement. She was reading him like a book.

"What Sir Graham means, Paul, is he wants *me* to pop over to Amsterdam . . . "

"But that's out of the question!" protested Temple.

"Why, darling? You don't think I'm sufficiently high-class goods?"

"It's not that," said Temple, staring angrily at Forbes. "This is a job for one of Sir Graham's women detective constables."

Forbes shook his head "They're excellent girls, Temple, but they haven't got Steve's – well, I don't know what to call it, style maybe."

"Yes, well I could never agree to it."

"You're not supposed to, darling. Go on, Sir Graham."

"There's absolutely nothing for you to worry about, Temple. You know Steve. When it comes to anything like this her head's not only screwed on, it's riveted on."

"What would you want me to do?"

"Well, pop over to Amsterdam as you put it and catch the same 'plane back as Mr Dordrecht. We'll try and get you the seat in front of him across the gangway. I should leave it to him to make all the running, which he will if his track record is anything to go on. But there's no harm in making sure he notices you. Then you just play it by ear. If he tries to make a date . . . "

"This just isn't on!" objected Temple, jumping up from his chair.

"Don't worry, Temple, I'll have half the Yard tailing her the moment she steps off the plane."

"Darling, I could do it standing on my head."

"What about her passport?" said Temple, clutching at straws. "If he sees the name Temple . . . "

"He won't. I've fixed that with the Foreign Office."

"Oh, you have?"

"She'll be travelling under the name of Gloria de Havilland."

"Gloria de Havilland. Mmm. I like that. Who on earth am I supposed to be?"

"A very up-market interior decorator." Forbes eyed the Temples' drawing-room, which of course had been styled by Steve. "I'll let you have the passport on Tuesday morning."

"Gloria de Havilland, Gloria de Havilland." Steve was trying the name out for size. "I love Amsterdam. Will I have time to do some shopping?"

Paul put a hand to his brow.

"No problem, Steve," said Sir Graham cheerfully. "We'll put you on an afternoon flight from Heathrow tomorrow. You can spend the night in Amsterdam, have a morning's shopping and be in plenty of time for your flight back. It's not late. Seven o'clock – Dutch time. Flight KL 123."

Paul had turned to the drinks cabinet in frustration. He poured himself a stiff whisky and drank it neat, casting dark looks over his shoulder at the other two.

Temple's ordeal began the moment he kissed Steve goodbye at London Airport. As always the flat without her seemed terribly empty. Charlie's efforts to cheer him up only made matters worse. He tried to get down to doing some work on his new book, but was quite unable to concentrate.

He had hardly finished dinner when the telephone rang. He just beat Charlie in the race to answer. It was Steve, 'phoning from her hotel bedroom.

"Yes, I have a lovely room overlooking the canal. Every-one's being very nice to me. I've been asked out to dinner by a very charming man. He's doing a research job for the European Commission."

"Not Dordrecht, by any chance?"

"Dordrecht is for tomorrow, darling. Now don't worry about me. I can take care of myself."

But of course he did worry, and slept badly that night. Though he knew her return flight was not till ten past five, London time, he stayed in all day, just in case. Forbes had promised that he would keep him informed of all developments from the moment Steve boarded the plane.

It was a quarter past five when Forbes made his first call from the operational headquarters he had set up at Scotland Yard.

"Everything is going as planned, Temple. They're both on the 'plane and it's taxiing out now."

"Have you a man on the 'plane?"

"Not necessary. We'll pick them up when they clear Customs."

"I still don't like it, Sir Graham."

After that call he paid a visit to the drinks cabinet but only for a glass of Malvern water. He wanted to keep a clear head.

The flight was due to land at Heathrow at seven o'clock. It was twenty-five past when Forbes telephoned.

"She's brought it off, Temple! They're sharing a taxi into town."

"You're following it?"

"Need you ask?" said Forbes and disconnected.

At eight twenty-five he rang to report that Steve and Dordrecht were at the Kensington Garden Hotel. They had both booked in and were having a drink in the cocktail bar.

"They're *both* booked in?"

"Yes, but separate rooms, don't worry."

Ten minutes later Forbes came through again to report that the pair had taken a taxi and were heading towards Mayfair.

"We'll keep this line open, Temple. Stay on call."

"Mr Temple." It was a nervous Charlie at the door. He had already discovered that his employer was excessively irritable. "I've cooked a nice steak for you—"

"Charlie, I'm busy! And I'm not hungry!"

Temple had laid the 'phone down on his desk so that his hands were free to unfold a map of Central London. He heard the words "Park Lane" and picked it up again. For three minutes he listened to the murmur of laconic police voices in the office at Scotland Yard.

Then Forbes' voice, loud in his ear, "You there, Temple? Their taxi has stopped at La Reserve Grill. I told you Dordrecht liked to do things in style."

"Can you get a man in there?"

"We'll certainly try!"

When confirmation came through that Steve and Dordrecht had been seated in the restaurant Temple relented and told Charlie to serve his meal.

Temple had finished his dinner by a quarter past nine. Steve and Dordrecht did not finish theirs till a quarter past ten.

At ten thirty, Forbes rang to report that Dordrecht had paid his bill and the pair were collecting their coats.

"Looks as if he's 'phoned for a radio cab. Taxis are at a premium this time of the night. Stay on call."

This time Temple did not put the phone down. He kept the earpiece tight against his ear. From the background noises he could hear there seemed to be a flap going on in the ops centre.

"Sir Graham! Sir Graham! Answer me, please!"

After an age the 'phone at the other end was picked up.

"Temple! We have a problem. I was right. He did 'phone for a taxi. We checked its number with the Police National Computer. It's a private vehicle, not a registered cab at all."

"Oh, God!"

"We're tailing it though. The driver's going like the wind . . . What's that, James? . . . " Forbes' voice had gone fainter for a moment. "The Cromwell Road? That could mean the M3 or the M4 . . . Temple, James and I are moving out! We'll establish a mobile HQ in a patrol car. I don't want to get left behind."

"Sir Graham, pick me up straightaway!"

"I don't want to do that, Temple. It might . . . "

"Straight away, Sir Graham!"

"Very well. Be outside your flat in five minutes!"

Temple could hear the squeal of tyres echoing round the streets of Belgravia before the unmarked police car came in sight and braked to a halt. A door at the back was opened. He scrambled in and the car shot away again.

Forbes and James were in the back seat. Two policemen sat in front. Both were bareheaded, with crisp haircuts. One concentrated on driving. The other kept up a continuous dialogue in the radio.

"Where are they now?" was Temple's first question.

Forbes did not answer. It was James who spoke up. "We've lost them."

Temple bit his tongue to stifle the explosion.

"He must have realised he might be tailed. He turned off at North End Road and got lost in a maze of little streets."

"We have the number though," Forbes tersely. "Every patrol car in the West London area has been alerted."

The police car driver had negotiated Sloane Square. Now he accelerated up Sloane Street, took a short cut through Beauchamp Place and joined the traffic flowing westwards on the Cromwell Road.

They had passed North End Road and crossed the Hammersmith Flyover when Forbes leant forward trying to interpret the series of jumbled quick-fire messages coming through on the radio. In a minute he'd have to choose whether to take the M3 or the M4.

"They've got him, sir." The radio operator half turned his head. "The M4. One of the Slough cars saw him turn off at Junction 5. He's taken the Datchet road."

"Let's get with them," said Forbes.

The driver put his foot down, expertly overtaking the stream of traffic moving at 60 mph. Over the Chiswick Flyover his speed went up to 90. Once on the motorway the needle reached the 140 mark and stayed there.

They reached Junction 5 in six minutes. The time was twelve seventeen. The radio operator turned round as the wind-roar died and the car lurched through the bends connecting the Datchet road to the motorway.

"Target has stopped just outside Windsor on the south side of the Thames. An observer reported that someone was carried on to a cabin cruiser moored to the bank."

"*Carried* !" Temple echoed. "That must mean Steve's either unconscious or—"

6   Just a Red Herring

Steve recovered consciousness to the steady beat of a diesel engine. She lay still, keeping her eyes closed, trying to figure out what had happened, tracking back in her memory.

Of course, it must have been that Irish coffee she'd asked for instead of a liqueur. It *had* tasted unduly sharp, she had begun to feel helplessly drowsy soon after Dordrecht had helped her into the taxi. He had parried her pleas to open a window and as the vehicle swung round Hyde Park Corner she had passed out.

She had to admit that Dordrecht had surprised her. Sir Graham had not exaggerated his good looks and charm. She had been aware of his scrutiny on the flight, but he had made no move till the passengers were walking up the long corridor to Customs and Immigration.

"Those bags look heavy. May I give you a hand?"

During dinner he had been charming, not too forward. He had shown interest in the life and work of Gloria de Havilland, without pressing her too closely on any point. When he asked for the bill, apologising that he had to have an early night, she was almost disappointed.

And now where was she? The slight movement and the beat of the engine told her that she was lying in a boat of some kind. She risked opening her eyes a fraction and saw that she was in a small cabin with two berths. A man she had not seen before was sitting on the other, reading an evening paper.

She had a splitting headache and was afraid that she was going to be sick. The smell of hot diesel was nauseating. She must have stirred unwittingly, for the man on the other bunk put his paper down. Keeping an eye on her, he went to the door, slid it open and called through to the other cabin.

"What's up, Bennet?" She recognised the voice as Dordrecht's.

"She's coming to," said Bennet nervously. "Don't you think we ought to gag her, if she screams—"

111

"Don't worry," said Dordrecht. "Come on, Pete. Now's your chance if you want to take a look at her."

Bennet did not re-enter the sleeping cabin but she saw the shadow of two other men. She closed her eyes again.

"She said her name was Gloria de Havilland." It was Dordrecht speaking. "And that she was an interior decorator. But her story did not stand up to a few well chosen questions. I became quite sure she was a plant, so I thought I'd better bring her along and see if we can make her talk."

"Gloria de Havilland? Do you know who this really is? Mrs Paul Temple!"

Steve's eyes had opened. She had been shocked into revealing herself by the sound of that voice. She found herself staring up into the face of Dr Elzec, the amiable Dane from the flat on the floor above them.

"Mrs Temple?" Dordrecht's jaw fell. He sat down on the bunk where the newspaper reader had been. "Did she know that I was travelling in that particular plane?"

"Of course I did!" said Steve with spirit. She realised her danger now that she had proof that Elzec was involved with Dordrecht in the counterfeit racket. She had to keep talking, and interestingly enough to prevent them gagging her.

"What was the point? How did you know that I was—"

"My husband found out."

"Found out what?"

"That you're mixed up in the counterfeit racket. The Dutch police have had their eye on you for weeks."

"You're lying," said Elzec quickly.

"I'm not lying."

"Then why didn't they arrest me?"

"Because," said Steve, gaining confidence, "the Dutch, like Scotland Yard, have got their priorities right. They're interested in Madison, not the small fry. They know you're only a glorified porter, used for smuggling the notes into Europe."

"You bitch!" Dordrecht's suave veneer had crumpled. "You've used me as a decoy!" His hand was raised to strike Steve but instead of smashing into her face his fist met the palm of Elzec's hand.

"I'm not having any of that," said Elzec. "She'll talk when we get to the cottage . . . "

Elzec broke off at the sound of a commotion overhead. Heavy feet pounded the deck just above them. The man they called Bennet shouted from the adjoining cabin. "We've been boarded! It's the police!"

Elzec ducked through the door. He slammed it behind him and turned the key. Steve filled her lungs and shrieked at the top of her voice, "Paul! Paul, I'm in—" Dordrecht's hand had clamped her mouth. As she bit it hard he yelled with pain and quickly snatched it away. Before he could come at her again she had coiled her legs. She was still wearing those high-heeled evening shoes. As Dordrecht's angry face leant over her she kicked hard, aiming at his throat. One heel met an arm, the other found his throat.

Dordrecht uttered a choking cry and clapped his hand to his throat. He was gasping for breath. Steve rolled quickly to the floor. As he swayed she seized the bottom of his trousers and yanked his legs from under him. Almost before he had finished falling across the bunk, she was on his back. The breath had gone out of him and she was able to put a lock on his arm. He was making a last desperate effort to free himself when Temple broke into the cabin.

The police launch was faster than the cabin cruiser but much less comfortable. Both boats were heading back down the Thames towards the jetties at Windsor, the launch on half throttle seeming to tow the cabin cruiser in its wake. Forbes, Temple and Steve were sitting in the tiny cabin behind the cockpit where a river policeman was at the wheel. Forbes had left James in charge of the cruiser with a couple of six-foot constables to help him. Elzec, Dordrecht, Bennet and a deck-hand called Harry were penned in the day-cabin.

"Feeling cold, Steve?" Forbes had seen Steve shiver.

"Just a bit."

"There's a greatcoat on the bench over there. She can borrow that."

Temple brought the coat and put it across her shoulders. Ahead, as they rounded a bend in the river, the outline of Windsor Castle showed up against the night sky.

"How on earth did you manage to find me, Sir Graham?"

"Thanks to the PNC and a favour from Lady Luck."

"Have you any idea where they were taking you?" asked Temple.

"I heard Elzec mention a cottage but I haven't the slightest idea where it is."

"When do you think Dordrecht rumbled you?"

"It might have been in the cocktail bar of the Kensington Garden Hotel. I made a slight slip there. Somebody hollered 'Steve' and my head jerked round. It was someone calling the waiter."

"That was bad luck." They could all laugh about it now.

"You've done a great job, Steve," Forbes congratulated her. "I'm sorry we lost you for a while, but things might have turned out worse."

"A lot worse!" agreed Steve, with feeling.

"But I've found out one thing, Paul. They both reacted to the name Madison . . ."

"Dordrecht was the courier obviously and I hope James has got that Samsonite suitcase we found in the cabin under his eye. I'll be interested to see what's . . ."

Temple's remark was punctuated by a deafening explosion. An orange flash came from the cabin cruiser and with it a blast that rocked the police launch and knocked all three of them flat. Temple was the first to pick himself up. When he looked back the cabin cruiser was settling lopsidedly in the water. The whole of one side had been blown out. He could just make out three or four figures struggling in the water.

"Is there anything in the paper about last night?"

"Just a late news flash. They refer to it as a mysterious explosion on the Thames in which three people lost their lives. There aren't any details."

"My goodness, I was lucky."

"Just how lucky I don't suppose you'll ever know."

Steve stared across the breakfast table at the patch of blue sky which was just visible above the tops of the houses. Even now she was not sleepy, though she and Paul had been able to snatch only a few hours in bed. She had been too stimulated by the previous evening's events to sleep properly and the narrowness of her escape gave her a heightened awareness of ordinary, everyday things – like the smell of good coffee, the flavour of bacon and eggs, the sight of her husband reading the morning paper.

The explosion that had ripped the side out of the cabin cruiser had not seriously damaged the launch of the river police.

They had turned back at once, the searchlight in the bow sweeping the water for survivors. Chief Inspector James had had a narrow escape. He had been on the far side of the boat and had been hurled into the water, but without serious injury. He had been the first one hauled into the launch, shocked and gasping for air. Detective Constable Smith had been clinging to a spar with his last ounce of energy; both his legs were shattered. Bennet had been pulled out of the water dead, though there was not a mark on his body. By contrast the deck-hand, Harry, was a bloody mess but still breathing. A second river police launch had come speeding up-river from Windsor. Forbes had decided to let them take over the search and rescue operation so that the injured could be taken back to Windsor and transferred to Casualty at the King Edward VII hospital. Temple was glad of the decision. He knew that Steve had been through enough and he wanted to get her back to the flat and under the care of the ever-protective Charlie. Forbes' driver had done the trip from Windsor to Eaton Square in twenty minutes.

"Paul."

"Yes, darling?"

"I'm glad you jumped us when you did – you know, instead of waiting."

"What are you talking about?"

"If you'd left me on the launch and simply followed us there's a sporting chance we should have taken you straight to their headquarters."

Temple lowered his paper and looked at her seriously. "You don't think I'd take a chance like that, do you?"

"Do you think James was right? That it was a time-bomb in the suitcase?"

"Either a time-bomb or a remotely-controlled device."

Temple made a wry face as the telephone shrilled insistently. It had been plugged into the dining-room and was standing on the side-board. "All right, I'll take it."

"Hello?"

"Is that Mr Temple?"

"Yes, who is that?"

"This is Moira Portland."

"Oh, hello, Miss Portland," Temple said reassuringly. Moira sounded very edgy. "I'm sorry, I didn't recognise your voice."

"Mr Temple, I don't want to be a nuisance, but do you think I could see you sometime? I'd like to talk to you . . . "

"Yes, of course. As a matter of fact I'd rather like to talk to you too."

"Could we – meet tonight?"

"Yes, certainly. Would you like to come to my flat?"

"No, I'd rather meet you at the Manila."

"We can talk much better here than at the Manila," Temple countered. For him the Manila Club had lost its charm.

"No. If I come to your flat I might be seen . . . "

"All right." Temple quickly changed his mind. "What do you want me to do – bump into you 'accidentally'?"

"Yes. I shall be there from nine o'clock onwards."

"Then I'll come about ten."

"Thank you. Oh, Mr Temple . . . "

Temple had almost replaced the receiver. Curbing his impatience he lifted it to his ear again. "Yes?"

"I'm awfully sorry I was rude to you at the weekend but you see I haven't been feeling very well recently and I'm afraid I've been rather overdoing things."

"Yes, I think you have, Miss Portland," Temple agreed crisply. "If I were you, I should go easy." He gave that a moment to sink in. "You know what I mean, don't you?"

"Yes. And there's something else I wanted to tell you." Temple waited, trying to make out from background sounds where she was calling from. He was pretty sure it was a call-box. "I – didn't – murder – Eileen . . . "

"I never thought you did."

"No, but the police think so, at least they will think so when they find . . . " Moira bit the sentence off. It sounded like a bait to draw Temple to the Manila.

"When they find what?"

"I'll tell you tonight."

"All right," Temple agreed patiently.

"And, Mr Temple. Whatever happens, please don't change your mind about me."

"What do you mean?"

"I – didn't murder Eileen, honestly I didn't. I'm just a red herring."

Temple put the 'phone down with a sigh, left his hand resting on it for a few seconds. "Well, what an extraordinary thing to say."

"What did she say? You seemed so surprised!"

"She said 'I didn't murder Eileen I'm . . . '" Temple frowned as Charlie knocked and opened the door. "What is it, Charlie?"

"There's a Mr George Kelly would like to see you, sir."

"Honestly," protested Steve, "some people seem to think we're a listening service."

"Yes, all right, Charlie." Temple swallowed what was left of his coffee. "Put him in the drawing-room."

Temple went into his study to fetch a small notebook, which he slipped into his pocket. When he reached the drawing-room he found Kelly biting a nail and looking out of the window down at the street. He had bought himself a new suit but its loud check pattern still gave the impression that he was dressed for some part in an old Hollywood musical.

Without preamble he launched straight into the reason for his visit.

"Mr Temple, I've been doing quite a lot of thinking during the past few days and I've reached a decision." Kelly paused, as if this was going to be the big saying of the week. "Do you know what I think? I think somebody's trying to make a monkey out of me."

"Make a monkey out of you?" repeated Temple politely, as if such a thought was inconceivable.

"Yes. Somebody impersonated me that night. I was supposed to have telephoned your wife at the Manila. Somebody tried to give you the impression that I was mixed up in this – what do you call it? – Madison affair."

"Aren't you mixed up in the Madison affair?"

"Most certainly not!" Kelly shook his head vehemently. "And I'll tell you another thing I'm not mixed up in either." He wagged a finger at Temple. "This Greene murder. Now, I don't know what your opinion is, Temple, but I've a hunch the police are trying to pin that rap on me."

Kelly had advanced round the sofa, still jabbing the air

117

with his finger. Temple withdrew a pace or two to avoid the whiff of stale whisky on the American's breath.

"The police aren't trying to pin a rap on anybody, as you so elegantly put it."

"Well, they've asked me an awful lot of questions – they keep on asking me an awful lot of questions."

"Does that surprise you?"

"Certainly it does. Why pick on me of all people? Why not pick on Hubert Greene, or Stella or Moira Portland for that matter?"

"You know how Eileen was murdered – she was stabbed."

"All right," Kelly conceded. "So she was stabbed. But does that mean that I stabbed her?" Kelly's brow wrinkled as his eyebrows went up. "Listen Temple, if I wanted to commit a murder would I use a knife? No sir, you bet your bottom dollar I wouldn't."

"What would you do, Mr Kelly?"

"Why—" Kelly was momentarily stumped for an answer to that question. "I'd shoot the guy or strangle him or something. I certainly wouldn't throw suspicion on to myself by using a dagger."

The two men had changed places. Temple was now at the window and Kelly was in front of the fireplace.

"Are you suggesting, then, that someone is deliberately trying to throw suspicion on to you?"

"I am. And what gets me is the fact that Scotland Yard can't see through it. I'm not mixed up in this Madison mystery, Temple. I'm just a red herring."

"I see. And is that why you came here this morning, Kelly, to tell me that you're just a red herring?"

"No, it isn't," said Kelly, with a faint air of triumph. "I came here because I wanted you to have a look at this brooch." He reached in his jacket pocket and produced a brooch, which he handed to Temple.

"Where did you find this?" Temple was turning the brooch over in his hands. It was a largish oval emerald, set in diamonds, with a clip instead of a safety pin.

"I came across it in the bushes, down by the lake, not so far from where you found Eileen Greene."

"Were you looking for it?"

"No. I went down to the lake that night because – well – I wanted to see the scene of the crime. I guess you can put it down to morbid curiosity. I was probing among the bushes when I found the clip. It's been rather badly knocked about, hasn't it?"

"Yes, I can see that. Why did you not hand this to the police?"

"Well," said Kelly innocently, looking Temple in the eye. "I've handed it to you, haven't I?"

"Have you any idea who it belongs to?"

"Yes, as a matter of fact I have." Kelly was smiling, enjoying keeping Temple in suspense. "It belongs to Moira Portland."

Big Ben was going through his preliminary chimes and booming the twelve strokes of mid-day over Westminster as Temple paid off his taxi in Victoria Street. It takes the big clock nearly a minute to strike mid-day and before it had finished he was at the reception desk of New Scotland Yard. Sir Graham had left a message that he was expecting him. Without delay he was whisked up in a lift to the sixth floor and admitted immediately to the inner sanctum.

"I'm afraid I'm a little late, Sir Graham."

Forbes glanced at the wall clock, which showed two minutes past the hour.

"That's all right. Greene hasn't arrived yet."

"Greene? Is that why you wanted me here?"

"Not exactly. As a matter of fact Greene made the appointment himself. I wanted to have a chat. Sit down."

The windows of Forbes' office looked out over Victoria Street. They were high enough to afford a view of Westminster Cathedral to the right and the Abbey on the left. Despite the regulation paint work and standard furniture the room reflected something of its occupant's personality. He had brought in his own big mahogany desk, and on one wall were Ackerman prints of his old school and Cambridge college. Another wall was occupied by a large-scale map of London divided into the various divisions and studded with a mass of colour-coded pins.

Temple sat in one of the two comfortable leather arm chairs. Forbes resumed his seat at his desk, behind a signed photograph of the Queen and Prince Philip.

"Temple, we don't seem to be getting anywhere with this

Greene murder. I had another talk with Kelly yesterday afternoon and he still sticks to his original story."

"Well, you've succeeded in rattling Mr Kelly if nothing else."

"Have you seen him?"

"Yes, he came to see me this morning. He produced this rather interesting trinket."

Temple stood up to put the emerald and diamond brooch on the desk.

"What is it – a clip?"

"Yes, apparently he found it by the lake near where Eileen Greene was found."

"Was that before or after the murder?"

"After. He says he went down there that night – out of ghoulish curiosity."

"It looks as if it's been trodden on. Why did he not hand this in to the police?"

"I asked him that. He said he'd intended to give it to me."

"I see," said Forbes, not too pleased. "Do you know who it belongs to?"

"Well, according to Kelly it belongs to Moira Portland, but personally I rather doubt it. Anyway, I'm seeing her tonight, I'll mention it. She asked me to meet her at the Manila."

"Why?"

"I don't know why – but I have my suspicions. Do you mind if I have it back?" Reluctantly Forbes pushed the brooch back across the desk. Temple put it in his pocket. "Any news of Elzec or the other man – Dordrecht?"

"We picked up Dordrecht shortly after you left us. There was no sign of Elzec."

"Was Dordrecht dead?"

"Yes." Forbes made the statement unemotionally. "So were Bennet and Sergeant Taylor – their bodies were picked up this morning."

"Oh, I'm sorry about that. Do you think Elzec was lucky and escaped or do you think there's still a chance of his being found?"

"I don't know." Forbes was cocking an ear to the sound of voices in the outer office. "According to James he was standing no more than a yard from him when the thing exploded. I'm inclined to think Elzec was thrown clear by the actual explosion."

"So he could have been drowned or he could have made it to the bank and got away across the fields?"

"If the frogmen don't find his body we must assume the latter. How's Steve this morning?"

"In remarkably good form, considering. You heard what she said about the cottage?"

"Yes, and I'm determined to find that place if it's the last thing I do."

"If you do find it you'll probably discover the whole set-up – the printing press and everything."

"Yes, I agree. Well, we're combing every inch of the river, Temple – we can't do more." The sound of voices had approached the door. Now there came a brisk knock and a plain clothes detective swung the door open. "Yes, Sergeant?"

"Mr Greene has arrived, sir."

"Right, send him in."

Hubert Greene was wearing a dark suit and an obviously new black tie. A lot of his self-confidence had vanished and there was an air of permanent tiredness about him.

"Come in, Greene," Forbes invited encouragingly.

"Good morning, Sir Gra—." He stopped, realising that Forbes was not alone. "Hello, Temple! I didn't expect to find you here."

"Would you like to see Sir Graham alone?" Temple offered.

"No, as a matter of fact I'm rather glad you're here."

"Won't you sit down?"

"Oh, thank you." Still nervous, Greene accepted Forbes' invitation and took the second armchair. He cleared his throat. "I'll tell you why I wanted to see you, Sir Graham. I've been thinking about last weekend, as a matter of fact I can't stop thinking about it. Sometimes, you know, it's difficult for me to realise that Eileen isn't . . . " He closed his eyes for a moment, and his mouth worked convulsively.

"Yes, I'm sure," said Forbes sympathetically.

"I'm staying in town as much as possible. I just can't bear the thought of going back to 'Brown Acres'. I had to go for the funeral, of course. It was kind of you to release the body, Sir Graham. I scattered her ashes on the lake there, Temple. I'm sure that's what she would have wanted."

"I can understand your feelings," Forbes said gruffly. He then decided that Greene had had his ration of condolences. "What did you want to see me about?"

"To tell you about something that happened, or rather something that was said the night before my wife was – murdered."

"Go on."

"We were in the library." Greene glanced at Temple, inviting him too to visualise the scene. "Stella, Eileen, Chris Boyer and myself. It was before Moira Portland and Mr and Mrs Temple joined us. I overheard a remark which Chris Boyer made to my wife. I didn't think anything about it at the time but in the light of what's happened I . . . " Greene's voice faltered again. He sought refuge in a study of his left palm.

"What did Boyer say to your wife?" Forbes prompted gently.

"He said, 'We'll have to talk about this, Eileen. We'll try and get together . . . ' "

Forbes let the words hang in the air. He was studying Greene carefully, watching his hands as well as his face.

"Have you any idea what he was referring to?"

"Not the slightest."

Temple caught Forbes' eye to indicate that he had a question. Forbes nodded imperceptibly.

"Was Boyer a friend of your wife's – a personal friend?"

"No." Greene turned to Temple to answer. "They hardly knew one another."

"Did you speak to your wife about what you overheard?"

"No, I didn't think it was important. In any case it went out of my mind. You remember what happened, Temple, Moira came down and we had that awful scene in the library." Greene rocked preparatory to heaving himself out of the deep chair. "I'm sorry to have bothered you, Sir Graham. I thought perhaps it might be important."

"It still might be important."

"Greene, tell me—" Temple had reached into his pocket for the brooch. "Have you seen this clip before?"

Greene did not take it. He gave it one quick look and shook his head positively. "No."

"You're sure?"

"Quite sure."

"It didn't belong to your wife, by any chance?" Temple persisted.

"No. No, I'm sure it didn't." Greene gave the object a second look. "I'd have known if she had anything like that."

Nothing much had changed at the Manila. The same bouncer checked Temple's brand new membership card and the same smiling girl exchanged his coat for a ticket. The place was emptier than last time Steve and Temple had been there, perhaps because it was earlier in the evening, perhaps because Thursday was not a very busy day. They were able to reach the bar without having to push their way through a crowd. But the steady beat of the loudspeakers in the basement disco still reverberated through all the rooms.

Temple was leading the way, searching for Moira Portland, when he saw a lonely and disconsolate figure drinking by himself at the bar. It was George Denson, the friend who had accosted Chunky Brooks with such bonhomie. He was slumped and dejected. He glanced up listlessly, knowing that the one face he wanted to see would not appear again. He recognised Temple at once and forced a wry smile.

"I met you that night you were here with Chunky, remember? Oh, good evening, Mrs Temple."

"Good evening, Mr Denson," Steve said, noting the deterioration in the man. "I remember you well."

"Terrible business, Temple." Denson shook his head. "I just can't believe Chunky's gone. He was the best pal anyone ever had. What can I get you to drink?"

"Well," Temple excused them, "we're supposed to be meeting someone. I can't see Moira, can you, Steve?"

"No. But isn't that Mrs Portland over there? I think she's seen us."

Steve was looking towards a small room, really more of a corridor, connecting the bar to the dining-room. A quartet of people were sitting over their cocktails, choosing their meal from the tabloid-sized menus the maitre d'hotel had given them. Stella Portland had excused herself from her companions and was coming towards the bar. She was still wearing black, but had chosen a dress that showed her remarkably well-preserved figure to advantage.

"Good evening, Mrs Portland," Temple greeted her, concealing his surprise.

"Good evening." Her smile embraced both Paul and Steve. "I didn't know you were members here."

At Stella Portland's approach George Denson had swivelled round on his bar stool, presenting his back. He was not in the mood to be introduced to middle-aged females.

"We're very new members. We only joined a couple of days ago. Would you care to have a drink with us?"

Stella Portland's smile was a fixture on her face. It was brave but unconvincing. Her sadness showed in her eyes. "Well, that's very sweet of you but I'm in a party and I can't break away so early in the evening."

"Well, later on perhaps."

"Yes, I'd love to."

"Is Moira in your party?" Steve inquired, her eyes woman-like, missing no detail of Stella's dress and adornments.

"Moira?" She seemed surprised. "No, as a matter of fact I haven't seen Moira since Eileen Greene's funeral. Did you know Hubert scattered her ashes on the lake at 'Brown Acres'? It was very moving . . . " She broke off, discountenanced by Steve's interest in her attire. "Is anything the matter with my dress, Mrs Temple?"

"I wasn't looking at your dress, Mrs Portland. I was looking at your clip."

"Oh?" Stella glanced down at the emerald brooch set in diamonds which she wore on her breast.

"It's charming, isn't it?"

"It is rather." Stella said, fingering it gently. "Sam bought it for me in New York . . . " Her smile had faltered for a moment. "As a matter of fact he bought me a pair but unfortunately . . . "

"You lost the other one," said Paul.

"Yes." She stared at him. "How did you . . . "

Temple had put a hand in his jacket pocket. He brought it out and held the clip in his palm. "Is this it?"

"Why, yes!" Stella caught her breath. "Wherever did you find it?"

"I didn't find it. Mr Kelly did."

"Where?"

"By the lake not very far from where Eileen Greene was murdered."

Stella looked from Paul's face to Steve's and back again. Her breast was rising and falling. "How very odd."

"Have you any idea where you lost it?"

"No, I'm afraid I haven't," she said vaguely.

Temple said quickly, "Mr Kelly was under the impression it belonged to Moira."

"Well, I can understand that." Stella took this statement calmly. "You see, I lent the clips to Moira and George must have seen her wearing them."

"When did you lend her the clips?"

"That night — the night before the murder. Don't you remember seeing them?"

"No, I can't say I do."

"I do!" Steve cut in. "She wore a black dress with a sort of ruffle across the top and a clip on each shoulder."

"That's right," said Stella, with a grateful look.

"Mrs Portland, let's get this straight." Temple's tone was uncompromising. "Did you lose the clip or did Moira lose it?"

"Well, I don't really know. You see, I lent her the clips and she returned them to me. Actually, she put them on my dressing-table when she went to bed. You remember she went up rather early that night . . . "

"Yes, I remember."

"Well, next morning I packed the clips — at least I think I did." Stella realised her explanation was not convincing, but she added briskly, "Anyhow, when I got back to town I found there was one missing." The smile was in place again. "Sorry to be so hazy about it, but that's what happened. May I?"

Before Paul was aware of what she intended to do, she had picked the clip off the palm of his hand and clenched it in her own.

"Now, if you'll excuse me, I think perhaps I'd better join my friends."

"We shall see you later," Temple promised.

"Yes, I hope so," she said sweetly and turned on her heel.

"Paul . . . "

"Yes, darling?" He was still staring at the retreating figure.

"Do you believe her story?"

"Well she seemed pretty hazy about it, didn't she? Come along, let's see if they have a table for us." He turned to Denson, but Chunky's friend was immersed in contemplation of his double scotch.

The couple were making their way towards the dining room when a young man came up the stairs from the discotheque. The music had momentarily halted. Even if he had wanted to he could not have avoided meeting them.

"Why, hello, Temple," he said, with apparent pleasure. "I've been expecting to see you, I hear you're a member now."

"Hello, Boyer," Paul said less enthusiastically. "Yes, we've both joined."

"That's fine. I'm glad to hear it." He turned his charm on Steve. "Well, and how are you, Mrs Temple?"

"I'm very well, thank you," said Steve, melted by the warmth of his greeting.

"Is Moira with you?" Paul enquired.

"No, as a matter of fact she's not here tonight."

"Will she be along later?"

"I doubt it," Boyer's eyes searched the throng in the bar. "She's usually here by this time if she's coming. I'm glad I bumped into you, Temple. There's something I wanted to ask you. Look, that table's free now." There were a few tables round the walls of the cocktail bar. Boyer had spotted a group standing up to go down to the disco. "Shall we sit down?"

"Why not?" Temple agreed. He and Steve followed Boyer to a table in the corner.

"I saw Inspector James this afternoon," Boyer said, when they were seated. "He came to my flat."

"Oh?"

"You know, Temple, I've got a hunch that the police think I'm mixed up in this business."

"What business?"

"Why the Greene murder."

"Whatever gave you that idea?"

"Well, James was very curious. He asked me a great many questions – some rather embarrassing ones, too."

"That isn't entirely unusual when a murder's being investigated."

A waitress had come to clear away the used glasses and take their order for drinks. Boyer waited till she had gone back to her post at the end of the bar.

"Look, I'd like to be frank with you about this business."

"By all means," said Paul with a faint smile.

"I know that this Greene case, the murder of 'Chunky' Brooks, the death of Mark Kendell, are all part and parcel of the same thing."

"Well?"

"Well, I want you to know I'm not mixed up in the Madison affair."

Temple was gazing at him steadily. His equable expression gave no hint that he was about to topple Boyer's confidence.

"Then tell me, why did you say to Mrs Greene, the night before she was murdered, 'We'll have to talk about this, Eileen. I'll meet you later tonight.' "

Boyer's chin dropped. He stared at Temple as if he could not believe his ears.

"What makes you think I said that?"

"You were overheard."

"Look here, if you think I'm behind any of this then you've got another think coming." Boyer's manner had completely changed. The easy charm had gone and there was a dangerous glint in his eyes. "It's perfectly obvious that somebody's trying to throw suspicion on me. You know what I am, don't you, Temple?"

"No. What are you, Boyer?"

"I'm just a red herring."

7   Four Suspects

"Mr Temple?" It was the bouncer who combined the roles of host, security officer, chucker-out and general factotum. "There's a call for you. You can take it in the telephone booth along the corridor."

Temple excused himself and went to the booth where Steve had taken the call purporting to come from George Kelly.

"This is James speaking. Temple, listen . . . don't leave the Manila. Sir Graham's on his way over. He wants to see you."

"What is it, James. Anything wrong?"

"It's Moira Portland . . . She's dead."

"Dead!"

"Yes, we found the body about twenty minutes ago."

"Where?"

"In Boyer's flat, just off Charing Cross Road."

"I see. Well, thanks for letting me know. I'll talk to Sir Graham when he arrives. Goodbye."

The waitress had brought the drinks by the time Temple rejoined Steve and Boyer at the table. Boyer had paid for them.

"Who was on the 'phone, Paul?"

"It was a message from Sir Graham. He wants to see me."

"Tonight?"

"Yes, he's calling here." Temple sipped his whisky and asked casually, "Boyer, when did you last see Moira Portland?"

"This afternoon, why?"

"I wondered, that's all."

Boyer knew that something lay behind Temple's question. "Look here, Temple, I think it's about time we cleared the air."

"By all means," Temple agreed calmly.

"What's your real opinion of me, Temple?"

"Well . . . "

"Come on, let's be frank. You've met me several times, we spent the weekend together down at Hubert Greene's place!"

Temple gave Boyer a long, considering look. "Well, the first time I met you, I thought you were a dim-witted young man who danced well. Now, I'm not so sure."

"Not so sure about what – my dancing?"

"No, that you are dim-witted. I think you are playing a part – and playing it very well, if I may say so."

"You may say so! And if it affords you any satisfaction you are the first person who spotted it." Boyer took a packet of cigarettes out of his pocket. "Before the Falklands War I was an actor. I did four years in weekly Rep and two years in the West End. That's when I first met Hubert Greene."

"Oh? Was he an actor too?"

"Yes, and a very good one. Especially in Shakespeare. But there wasn't enough money in it for him." Boyer laughed. "Not for me either. I suppose to satisfy a craving for something more active I joined the Territorial Army. When the Falklands was invaded I was called up to join the Task Force as an Intelligence Officer. It so happens I speak four languages, including fluent Spanish."

Boyer paused to light his cigarette. There was a faraway look in his eyes and Temple guessed that his memories of the South Atlantic were not all rosy.

"Go on . . . "

"When the campaign was over I came back to the theatre – brimming with enthusiasm. After eighteen months I was eventually offered a part in a French farce. I had three lines. I stuck it for almost twelve months and then one night I decided to change my tactics. I'd always been a good dancer and women were never exactly allergic to me. The rest you can guess."

That Boyer was an actor was evident. Indeed he was more of an actor in his real life than on stage. But now he had dropped the mask and a completely different character was revealed.

Steve had been watching the transformation with fascination. Now she asked, "And how does Moira Portland fit into the picture?"

"She doesn't," Boyer stated bluntly.

"What do you mean?"

"I broke off our engagement this afternoon, Mrs Temple. You see, I quite enjoy playing the part of a deb's delight but . . ."

"You don't like to be called a well-dressed layabout – at least, not to your face?"

"Exactly."

Boyer looked round to see if this conversation was being overheard. But everyone else in the bar was absorbed with their own partners and in any case the general hubbub would have made it impossible to eavesdrop.

"Is that the real reason you broke off your engagement?"

"What other reason could I have?"

"The fact that she's on hard drugs?"

Boyer drew deeply on his cigarette. "When did you discover that?"

"I guessed it," said Temple, "the night she pretended to be drunk."

"Moira's changed a great deal during the past few months. I don't know why but she seems worried and almost – almost frightened at times."

"Have you any idea what she's frightened about?"

"No, I haven't, but curiously enough Chunky Brooks must have noticed something too – he asked me a great many questions about Moira. He spoke to Eileen Greene about her as well. That was the significance of the remark – the one that Greene overheard that evening at 'Brown Acres'. I wanted to have a word with Eileen about it and simply said – 'We'll have to talk about this, Eileen. I'll meet you later tonight.'"

"And did you meet her?"

"Of course not." Boyer's eyes flashed resentfully. "She was murdered, you know that!"

"You said just now that Hubert Greene overheard your remark – how do you know it was Greene?"

"You said so!"

"No, I didn't," Temple contradicted him. "I simply said your remark was overheard."

"Well," said Boyer angrily. "I took it for granted it was Greene."

"Here's Sir Graham," said Steve, who had her back to the wall and could see the entrance to the cocktail bar. She gave a wave to attract his attention.

Sir Graham was an incongruous figure in the context of the Manila Club. He was wearing a long tweed coat with a dark brown velvet collar and carried his hat in his hand. The cloakroom girl had not been able to persuade him to part with any of his accoutrements. Many pairs of eyes were on him as he crossed the room to the table in the corner and a momentary hush fell. Politely he borrowed a chair from a nearby table and sat down between Temple and Boyer.

"Did you get my message, Temple?"

"Yes, James rang me."

"Have you said anything to—" he nodded at Boyer.

"No. Actually we were just discussing Moira."

Boyer had been watching the two men intently. The nod had not escaped him.

"Has anything happened, Sir Graham?"

The hum of conversation had risen again, but all the same Forbes lowered his voice. "Yes, Boyer, I'm afraid I've got some very bad news for you."

"Is it Moira?"

"Yes – she's committed suicide."

"Oh no! I was afraid of that." Boyer was not acting now. His distress was unfeigned. "How did it happen?"

"She gassed herself." Forbes paused before adding "In your flat, Boyer. Apparently she let herself into the flat about eight o'clock." He stared at Boyer, who was too shocked to speak. "Did you know she had a key?"

"What?"

"I said, did you know she had a key?"

"Yes, I gave it to her."

"There's no doubt that it was suicide, Sir Graham?" Temple asked.

"No doubt." Forbes did not even look at Temple to answer the question. "Boyer, what did you mean just now when you said 'I was afraid of that'?"

"Well, Moira's been very strange lately. She's been terribly overwrought and at times quite impossible to talk to. As a matter of fact I was talking to Temple about it only a few minutes ago."

"Mr Boyer was saying that he'd just broken off his engagement."

"Oh! When did that happen?"

"This afternoon."

"Was Miss Portland upset?"

"We were both upset," said Boyer and added drily. "It wasn't exactly a pleasant afternoon."

"Where did you see her?" Forbes asked.

"At her flat. I arrived about a quarter to three and left just after four."

"Did anyone else call on her while you were there?"

"No, but there was a 'phone call."

"Who was it, do you know?"

"Yes, it was Mrs Portland."

"Did you hear the conversation?"

"Part of it. They seemed to be making an appointment to see each other."

Forbes leant back in his chair and exhaled his breath. "Well, we can soon check on that."

"She's here, Sir Graham," Steve said.

"What? Here—at the Manila?"

"Yes, we were talking to her a few moments ago. She may have gone through to the dining-room. She was with a party."

"Boyer, would you mind asking Mrs Portland if she can spare me a moment?"

Boyer nodded and got up from the table. He was probably quite glad of a respite from Forbes' relentless questions.

"Oh, dear, poor girl," said Steve. "Why do you think she did it, Sir Graham? Because Boyer broke off the engagement?"

"I don't think the engagement had anything to do with it. She'd been taking cocaine—did you know that, Temple?"

"I know she was on hard drugs. What can I get you to drink, Sir Graham?"

The waitress had disappeared, so Temple had to go to the bar himself to fetch Forbes a large brandy. When he returned to the table Forbes was answering a question from Steve.

"A woman went to see Moira this afternoon just after Boyer left her — from the description we've received it sounds remarkably like Mrs Portland."

"Well, that rather ties up with the 'phone call, doesn't it?"

"Yes. Oh, thank you." Forbes looked up as the balloon-shaped glass was put down in front of him. "You know,

Temple, we've got four first-class suspects in this Madison mystery."

"Who are the four?" Steve started to count them on her fingers. "Stella Portland, Hubert Greene, George Kelly . . . "

As she paused Temple supplied the fourth name. "And Chris Boyer."

"But you said that you didn't think he had anything to do with Moira committing suicide."

"Exactly," Forbes stated crisply and clammed up. He had seen Boyer coming across the room alone.

"Mrs Portland suggests we move into the ante-room," he told Temple. "It's quieter there."

The four of them picked up their glasses and carried them into the smaller bar adjoining the dining-room. It was empty now, last orders having been taken and the diners having moved into the restaurant. Empty, that is, except for Stella Portland, who was sitting alone on one of the couches. It was evident from her face that Boyer had already broken the news to her.

"Sir Graham, is this true what Chris has just told me about Moira?"

"Yes, I'm afraid it is, Mrs Portland."

"Oh the silly, stupid girl! Whatever made her do it? I told her that . . . " She bit back a sob.

Forbes had decided after all to take off his overcoat. He dropped it over a chair and sat down facing her across a low table. "Mrs Portland, when did you last see your step-daughter?"

Stella had been watching as Steve, Paul and Boyer took chairs close to her, so that she was surrounded on all sides.

"What did you say?"

"I said," Forbes repeated his question with icy distinctness, "when did you last see your step-daughter?"

"Oh, er – several days ago. As a matter of fact I haven't seen her since the weekend."

"You didn't call on her this afternoon?"

"No – I've told you, I haven't seen her for several days."

"Did you speak to her on the telephone?" Forbes persisted.

"No I—" For the first time Stella met his eye and what she saw there warned her. Abruptly she changed her tack. "Yes I did. I spoke to her this afternoon."

"Did she ring you or . . . "

"No, I rang her. I wanted to arrange" – she glanced at Boyer – "a luncheon date."

"Did you arrange it?"

"Yes – for next Friday."

Forbes picked his glass up, cupped his hand under it and expertly rotated the brandy. "Mrs Portland, you must forgive me if I ask you a rather personal question . . . "

"I'm getting quite used to personal questions, Sir Graham," said Stella, with a flash of her old good humour.

"How did you get on with your step-daughter?"

"As a matter of fact, I got on quite well with her. I don't expect you to believe that, but the fact remains, I did! When we first met we took an instant dislike to one another and then gradually things began to change. I think she realised that I was a friend not an enemy."

"Had she many enemies?"

"I should ask Mr Boyer that question. After all, he was her fiancé."

Temple said, "Boyer broke off the engagement this afternoon."

"Broke off the . . . " The look Stella gave Boyer was both shocked and angry.

"Didn't you know that?"

"No, I didn't," she said, still fixing Boyer with her eyes.

"What was Moira like on the phone?" Temple asked. "Did she sound worried or depressed at all?"

"No more than usual. She hadn't a lot to say. I had the impression there was someone with her."

"I was with her," Boyer stated.

"Oh." Stella shook her head, like a boxer who has been punched once too often.

"Have you any idea why she committed suicide?" asked Forbes.

"No, I haven't unless it was the breaking of her engagement?"

That did not satisfy Forbes. "You can't think of any other reason why she should have taken her life?"

"No . . . " Steve felt almost sorry for Stella as she stared at Forbes obviously distressed. "No, I can't."

"I think you can, Mrs Portland, if you try."

The Temples did not linger at the Manila that evening.

After hearing the news of Moira's suicide and Forbes' grilling of her step-mother Steve had not felt like dancing. The bouncer whistled up a taxi for them and they were home soon after eleven. Temple had seen from the street that all the lights in the front rooms of the flat were on.

"Perhaps Charlie thought we wouldn't be home till late and decided to throw a party. I wouldn't put it past him, would you, Paul?"

Temple withdrew his key from the lock. "I think we'd better ring the bell. I wouldn't want to catch him *in flagrante delicto*."

As the buzzer sounded inside the flat Steve was staring at the mat outside the door.

"That can't be a drop of blood, Paul? It's still wet."

Paul stooped to examine the glistening stain. He touched it with a finger and put the finger to his nose. "By Timothy! It *is* blood! I wonder if Charlie's had an accident."

This time Temple did not wait. He put his key in the lock and opened the door. To his relief he saw Charlie coming across the hall.

"Sorry I couldn't answer the door, Mr T. I was in the bathroom helping Mr Kelly tidy up."

"Mr Kelly?" said Steve.

"What's happened, Charlie?"

"Mr Kelly's 'ad a bit of a rough house. E's been tidying up in the bathroom."

Steve was on Temple's heels as he strode into the bathroom. George Kelly had his head over the basin. He raised it and turned round when he heard footsteps. His face was bruised, the skin torn in several places. The water in the basin was pink and flecked with blood. He had taken his jacket off and thrown it on the floor.

"Hello!" he greeted them with remarkable cheerfulness. "Say, I'm glad you're back."

"What on earth have you been up to?"

"You might well ask!"

"Have you been in a fight?"

"I've been in a fight all right, I don't know what happened. It seemed to me I was hit by a hurricane. One minute I was standing on my feet – the next I was fighting for dear life." Kelly stared with concern at the battered face in the mirror. "Just look at my face! Uncle Sam certainly took an awful beating."

"Suppose you start at the beginning. What are you doing here, anyway?"

"Well, I was passing your apartment so I thought I'd drop in for a few minutes."

Temple ostentatiously looked at his watch "It must have been well after eleven."

Kelly ignored the comment. "The elevator was on the top floor and I rang for it."

"Well?"

"Well, it came down. The light wasn't on so I took it for granted it was empty, but just as I put my hand on the gate it was thrown open and – wham! For a moment I just didn't know what had hit me."

"You mean to say someone stepped out of the lift and deliberately hit you?"

"Hit me!" Kelly gingerly rubbed his chin. "He certainly did!"

"But why?"

"Either the guy was nuts or he didn't want me to see him. Anyway, we went at it hell for leather. Suddenly he landed me a real Mike Tyson – and when I recovered the guy had disappeared."

"Would you recognise him again?"

"No, I don't think I would. You see, we were more or less in the dark and the whole thing happened so quickly."

"All right, Kelly," said Temple, "join us when you're ready. I daresay you can do with a whisky."

"And how!"

"You know, Kelly, that's rather a remarkable story of yours."

Now that he had a large Scotch in his hand Kelly was feeling a lot better. Thanks to Charlie's styptic pencil the cuts and contusions on his face had stopped bleeding. He had a plaster over one eyebrow and another on his chin. Charlie had rifled Temple's dressing-room to provide him with a shirt to replace the torn, bloodstained one. It was far too big, but as he was not wearing a tie that did not matter.

"Remarkable? It's fantastic! If I was in your shoes I just wouldn't believe a word of it."

"You're quite sure you wouldn't recognise the man again?"

"I'm quite sure."

Temple was pouring himself a whisky. He added a generous measure of water. "Anyway, sit down and tell me what you wanted to see me about."

Kelly sat down and cradled the glass in his lap. "Well – you know that brooch, or rather clip, I found – the one I handed over to you this morning?"

"Yes?"

"I've been thinking about that. Maybe that was a tactless thing for me to say when I found the brooch very near the spot where Mrs Greene was murdered."

"Why tactless?"

"Well, I don't want to throw suspicion on to Moira Portland. I don't want to throw suspicion on to anybody."

"Don't worry, you won't throw suspicion on Miss Portland. You see, Kelly – she's dead. She committed suicide."

"You don't mean it! When?"

"Earlier this evening."

"A young kid like that, why . . . " The glass in Kelly's hand shook. "Whatever made her do such a stupid thing? What made her do it?"

"Your guess is as good as mine. It might even be better."

On the low table beside the fireplace the telephone had started to ring. Temple rose to answer it. "Excuse me." Temple put the phone to his ear, said, "Hello?"

"Temple? . . . This is Elzec." The voice was no more than a croak.

"Dr Elzec . . . ?"

"Temple, listen . . . There's something I . . . must tell you . . . " He was clearly finding it very difficult to talk. Each phrase was punctuated by a gasp.

"Elzec, what's happened?"

"I've been . . . attacked, knifed . . . I . . . I . . . "

"Elzec! Where are you . . . ? Can you hear me?"

"Yes . . . can hear you . . . " He broke off to cough. "Want to see you . . . the cottage at Lockdale . . . going there the night . . . night Madison double-crossed us . . . "

"Elzec, listen!" Temple said urgently "Where are you? Where are you speaking from?"

"I'm upstairs . . . in the flat . . . You'd better . . . be quick . . ."

Temple heard a clatter, as if nerveless fingers had dropped the receiver. He slammed his own instrument down. Kelly was already on his feet. The glass in his hand had been emptied.

"What is it? What's happened?"

"Elzec's been stabbed! He's in the flat above. Come on, Kelly, quick!"

The lift was at the ground floor. Temple did not waste time summoning it. He took the stairs to the top landing three at a time, with Kelly panting in his wake.

He knew that there would be no point in ringing the bell, and trying to fiddle the lock would take too long. His eye fell on a cylindrical fire extinguisher standing in the corner of the top landing. Filled with liquid it was as heavy as the barrel of a small cannon.

"Come on, Kelly, give me a hand. We'll use this as a battering ram. Aim just below the lock."

The two men hefted the extinguisher to shoulder height and swung it against the door. The sound boomed down the stair-well. Luckily the key of the mortice lock had not been turned and the door had only closed on the latch. At the third impact it gave way and the door shuddered open.

Temple was first in, groping for the switches in the darkened flat. When the sitting-room lights came on they revealed overturned chairs and tables, scuffed-up floor mats, smashed lamps and ornaments.

"Gee, what's hit this place?" Kelly had come into the room behind Temple. "There's been a whale of a fight by the looks of things."

The sitting-room telephone was still on its cradle. It was one of the few objects that had escaped damage. Temple was looking for an instrument that had been dropped to the floor.

He found it when he went through to the bedroom, although the receiver itself was not visible. It lay beneath the body that had slumped to the floor. The concertina connecting-wire led to a wall socket by the bed. A trail of blood led across the bedroom. Elzec must have used his last ounce of strength to crawl to the telephone. Gently Temple turned him over. The head rolled back. Like Chunky Brooks he had been stabbed repeatedly.

"I'm afraid we're too late, Kelly."

"Gee, that's terrible!" Kelly looked at the face once then turned away quickly. "Temple, you know that character I bumped into. He's responsible for this! He murdered Elzec!"

Temple had freed the telephone and got a dialling tone. He stabbed the number 9 three times.

"It's possible, quite possible . . . " he murmured.

"Emergency. Which service?" came the operator's voice.

"Ambulance first, then police."

Steve could usually read Temple's mind very well, but this morning he had her really guessing. In spite of the terrible events of the previous evening he appeared to be in a remarkably good mood. She was certain that he had something up his sleeve but she knew better than to try and prise it out of him. She did as he asked and made herself ready to go out, exactly as if she had a date to meet some friends for coffee. When she had chosen a handbag and inspected herself in the mirror she went to the study.

Temple looked up from his desk with genuine admiration.

"I say, you do look glamorous!"

"Well, I don't feel glamorous! Look, have I got to go out this morning?"

"Yes, Steve, you have. And don't forget what I told you!"

"Paul, do you really want me to do that?"

"I do."

"But it doesn't make sense."

"Doesn't it, darling?" Temple was still contemplating her with a pleased expression.

"Well, don't worry about it."

The door opened and Charlie appeared.

"I'm off now, Mr Temple."

"All right, Charlie. Have a good time."

"And where do you think you're going?" Steve demanded.

"I'm having the day off," grinned Charlie.

"Oh, you are, are you?"

Steve looked from Charlie to Temple, more than ever suspicious.

"S'right. Mr Temple said it'd be O.K."

"That's all right, Charlie," Temple told him. "Run along!"

When the door closed Steve faced her husband across the desk. "Now look here, Paul, I don't know what's going on here this morning, but I intend to find out."

Temple was spared the need to answer by the reappearance of Charlie.

"Here's Chief Inspector James to see you, sir," he announced briefly.

As Charlie vanished again Temple came out from behind his desk to greet the visitor.

"Why, hello, Inspector. Come in!"

"Good morning, Mrs Temple," James greeted Steve respectfully.

"Good morning, Chief Inspector," she replied, a little severely, though it was hardly James' fault that he had interrupted her inquisition. "I'll be on my way now, Paul."

"Yes, all right, darling. Don't forget what I told you."

Steve did not deign to answer and a few seconds later the front door banged for the second time.

"Come along, James, let's go into the drawing-room."

To Temple's relief James declined a coffee, but asked permission to light his pipe. His face showed the strain that comes inevitably with a murder investigation. He had spent another night without sleep.

"Well, how did you get on upstairs?" Temple asked, with a glance at the ceiling.

"It'll be another day before we finish going over the flat. You made a fine mess of the door."

"Anything to go on so far?"

"Very little of the stuff seems to belong to Elzec. It's mostly Major Hartley's."

"Finger prints?"

James shook his head. "We're working on it. Elzec must have inflicted damage on his attacker. We may get something from his knuckles and finger nails. But that's not why I wanted to see you."

Temple waited for the question.

"Are you quite sure that Elzec said: 'the cottage at Lockdale'?"

"Yes."

"It was Lockdale?"

"Yes, I'm sure. Why?"

"Well, if there's a cottage down there being used for this counterfeit racket then we've yet to find it."

Temple had moved to the window. Drawing the curtain back he was just in time to see Steve cross the street and walk briskly away towards Sloane Square.

"Well, I'm sure Elzec said Lockdale."

"All right, we'll go on checking. We'll move the whole of Scotland Yard down there if necessary." James pressed the tobacco in his pipe down and applied another match. "Temple, you remember that fellow Mark Kendell – the chap who broke into your flat?"

"Yes."

"I've got a theory about him. I think that Kendell was under the impression that Elzec was double-crossing him. It's my opinion that he didn't intend to break into your flat that night, but into Elzec's."

"In other words, he picked the wrong flat?"

"Exactly. Don't forget Elzec had only moved in the day before."

Temple nodded. "That would explain a lot."

"And there's another point, Temple. You remember that explosion on the river?"

"I shan't easily forget it."

"Well, I think I know what happened that night. Madison took a suitcase down to the launch, he told Elzec it was something for the cottage. But in fact it was a bomb. Either the suitcase contained a timer, or the device could have been triggered by a radio signal. I think that Madison wanted to get rid of Elzec, Dordrecht and the rest of the gang."

"In other words he's going into liquidation?"

"Exactly."

"You may be right, Inspector. If you are . . . We've got to move fast."

"Temple, what do you think happened last night?"

"Upstairs? It's only a theory, but try this for size. Elzec realised that Madison had tried to kill him. He let Madison know that he was still alive and lured him to the flat last night. He intended to have a show-down, possibly threaten Madison with exposure. But he forgot that he was dealing with a savage murderer – who had struck three and

141

perhaps four times already. Faced with a maniac Elzec did not stand a chance."

James looked up at the ceiling. "Must have been a hell of a fight. Funny you did not hear anything."

"We had not got back from the Manila and you can bet Charlie had his television on full blast."

"And Kelly was beaten up by Madison who was making a getaway after the attack on Elzec?"

"Yes, I'm inclined to believe Kelly's story."

Outside in the hall the buzzer had sounded. Someone was at the front door.

"That's one theory, of course," said James. "There is another."

But Temple was not interested in the other theory. "What time is it?"

"It's just gone twelve."

"I think that's George Kelly at the door, will you excuse me?"

"Oh, I'd like a word with Kelly," James said with satisfaction.

"Well, I did rather want to see him alone . . . " Temple pointed out with some embarrassment.

"I can wait." James eyed the chairs, trying to decide which one would be most favourable for a short cat-nap.

"No, I'd—" Temple seemed secretly amused, "er – prefer you to see him some other time, if you don't mind."

James' eyes narrowed. He took his pipe out of his mouth and aimed the stem at Temple. "Are you up to something, Temple?"

"I'll take him into the study and you slip out the front door."

"What's going on here?" James was now really suspicious. "Why shouldn't I see Kelly?"

Temple decided to change his tack. Very formally he said, "No reason at all, if you really want to."

James stared at him, trying to read what was going on in his mind. Temple gazed back at him levelly.

"All right, Temple. You play it your own way." James put his pipe into his pocket. "I'll slip out when you're in the study."

"Thanks, Inspector."

Kelly had pressed the bell push twice before Temple

opened the door to him. He still bore the marks of the previous night's fight. The plaster had been removed and dried scabs showed where his skin had been broken. His experience had not suppressed his habitual cocksureness.

"Sorry I was out when you 'phoned," he said, slipping into the hall. "I only got your message about an hour ago."

"That's all right. I'm glad you could make it."

Temple moved to shepherd Kelly away from the closed door of the drawing-room.

"Let's go into the study."

Kelly threw the newspaper he was carrying onto a chair. On the threshold of the study he stopped.

"Say, this is some den!"

"Do you like it?"

"I certainly do." Kelly's eyes were doing a tour of the room, taking in the dictating-machine, photo-copier, word processor. "Is this where you write all those books?"

"Well, most of them. Would you like a glass of sherry?"

"Yeah — I think maybe I would."

"It's very dry, is that all right?"

"Can't be too dry for me." Kelly had moved to stand in front of the case which contained all Paul Temple's titles. "Say, you've written some books, Temple!"

"One or two," said Temple from the small cabinet where he kept a decanter and some glasses.

"Do you know, funny enough, I've never read one of yours."

"There's nothing funny about it," Temple said with a smile. "A great many people haven't read my books."

"I go in for Westerns. You know the sort of thing. *Riders Over Arizona, The Sheriff of Melton Creek.*"

"Shades of Zane Gray." Temple handed Kelly a schooner of Manzanilla. "Well, your very good health."

"And yours." Kelly raised his glass in reply. He took a good drink and smacked his lips in appreciation.

"Sit down, Kelly." Temple waved Kelly to an easy chair and sat down behind his desk. "I'll tell you what I wanted to see you about. I've been having a talk with Chief Inspector James. He's got a theory about last night. He thinks that Elzec was murdered by a man called Madison and that it was Madison who bumped into you coming out of the lift."

"Well, that's exactly what I thought," Kelly said indignantly. "I told you."

"Of course you did," Temple said soothingly. "Well, he'd like you to go down to the Yard and look at some photographs. You might be able to pick him out."

"What – the man who attacked me?"

"Yes."

Kelly shook his head decisively. "There's not a hope. I wouldn't recognise him if he walked into this room. I told you, it was dark. I hardly saw the guy."

"All the same, we'd like you to have a look at the photographs . . . Excuse me." On the desk the telephone had started ringing. Temple picked the receiver up, pressed the earpiece close to his head so that Kelly would not hear the caller's voice.

"Well, here I am, darling," said Steve brightly. "You told me to ring up."

"Oh, hello, Steve!" said Temple, as if he had not seen his wife for hours.

"Well, don't sound so surprised."

"Is anything the matter, darling?"

"No, of course there isn't anything the matter! Remember you told me to . . . "

"I say, that is too bad," said Temple sympathetically "Where did it happen?"

"Where did what happen?" Steve asked, puzzled by the question.

"Have you tried waiting for ten minutes and then trying the starter again?"

"Paul, what are you talking about?" Steve was beginning to sound really cross. Paul pressed the receiver tighter against his ear.

"Oh, Steve, you probably gave it too much choke. It's no good gunning the starter, you'll only end up with a flat battery. Where are you? Where are you speaking from?"

"Where do you think I'm speaking from? I'm in the call box at the end of the road. That's where you told me . . . "

"Look Steve, I'd better come down. Go back and sit in the car, darling."

"I haven't got the car, Paul. I walked down to the box."

"Yes, all right. You stay where you are. I shan't be long, darling." Cutting off protestations, Temple hung up.

"Is anything wrong?" Kelly asked anxiously. He'd been trying to make sense of Temple's end of the conversation.

"Yes, my wife's having trouble with the car. Not exactly an unusual occurrence." Temple stood up. "Would you mind if I popped out for five or ten minutes? I'd better give her a hand."

"Sure," said Kelly, standing up also. "I'll come with you."

"No, as a matter of fact I'd rather you didn't. The flat's empty and I'm expecting a call from Scotland Yard."

"Do you want me to take it?"

"I'd be grateful if you would. It'll be Sir Graham Forbes. Tell him I'll see him as arranged — nine o'clock tonight."

"O.K. I'll do that."

"I shan't be long. Help yourself to the sherry."

During the forty minutes Temple had been absent Kelly had taken the invitation to help himself to the sherry literally. The level in the decanter had gone down by several inches. Kelly was sprawled in the arm chair reading one of the Paul Temple novels he had taken from the book-case.

"I hope you helped yourself to the sherry," Paul remarked drily.

"Yeah, I nearly started on the whisky." Kelly stood up and slid the book back into the shelf.

"You should have, Mr Kelly," said Steve "It would have taught my husband a lesson. Leaving you alone in the flat like that."

"Did anyone call?"

"No, and no one 'phoned either."

"Oh — didn't Sir Graham ring?"

"No," said Kelly, gently touching a cut on his forehead.

"That's funny." Temple went behind his desk and made a gesture of annoyance. "How stupid of me! I forgot to switch the ansaphone off." He reached over and pressed one of the buttons.

Kelly asked, "What was the matter with the car, Mrs Temple?"

Temple laughed. "Tell him, darling."

"I will not."

"She ran out of petrol."

"Oh, that's too bad." Kelly said with male chauvinistic

sympathy. "Well, I'm afraid I've got to be making a move. I've got a date."

"Well, look here, Kelly, please do drop into the Yard and have a word with James. I'd like you to check on those photographs."

"O.K. But I've told you it's no use. I'm sure I shouldn't recognise the guy again."

"Well, you never know. If you can give James some idea of the height and build of the man who attacked you . . . "

"Goodbye, Mrs Temple." Kelly was already in the hall.

"Goodbye, Mr Kelly."

No sooner had the front door closed than Steve's manner changed. Temple came back into the study to find her facing him angrily.

To mollify her he said, "I'd forgotten how attractive you look in that dress . . . "

"Now, look here, Paul – don't start giving me the run around."

"The run around?" Temple echoed innocently.

"Yes, the run around. Now what's this all about?" In her anger Steve was pacing the space in front of the desk. "First of all you give Charlie the day off, then you make me go down to the call box and put through a phoney 'phone call, then you invite Mr Kelly to the flat and leave him high and dry . . . "

"Hardly dry, darling! Look at the sherry!" Temple was obviously enjoying his little mystery. "Don't you know what it's all about?"

"Of course I don't know what it's all about!"

On the desk the telephone had started to ring.

"Well, where's that intuition of yours?"

"You keep my intuition out of this," Steve snapped.

Temple had reached the telephone. He scooped the receiver off its cradle.

"Hello?"

"Is that you, Temple?"

"Who is that?"

"This is Hubert Greene."

"Oh, hello, Greene."

Steve made as if to leave the room, but Paul motioned her to stay.

"Temple, I'm awfully sorry I couldn't make it this morning."

"Make it? Make what?"

"I got your note last night. You said would I call round and see you at twelve o'clock this morning."

"My dear fellow, I never sent you a note."

"But I've got it here – in front of me."

"I sent you a note asking you . . . "

"Asking me to call round at twelve o'clock this morning – yes." Greene was trying to control his irritation at Temple's obtuseness. "Unfortunately I was kept at the office and couldn't make it."

"But Greene, I tell you I didn't send you a note."

"But—" said Greene impatiently. "I've got it here in front of me."

"Maybe you have, but the fact remains that I didn't send it."

"Then who did?"

"Was the note posted?"

"No, it was delivered by hand. I found it in the letter box."

"Well, bring it round to the flat this evening. You know where to find me. Shall we say nine o'clock?"

"Yes, all right, I will. Goodbye."

"What did he want, Paul?" Steve asked, curious in spite of herself. "Something about a note?"

"Greene received a note asking him to call here at midday. He apparently couldn't keep the appointment because he was detained at the office."

"Did you send him the note?"

"No."

"Then who did? Do you know?"

"I've got a very good idea," said Temple.

The Temples were left in peace for the next half hour. Appetising smells were coming from the kitchen where Steve was preparing tagliatelle alla bolognese. Temple was in his study, rewinding the tape in his ansaphone. He had just finished when he heard the front door buzzer.

"I'll go," he called to Steve in the kitchen.

"Lunch is nearly ready," she warned him. "I don't want it spoiled."

"Don't worry, I'll get rid of them." But when he opened the door he forgot about lunch.

Stella Portland was almost in a state of nervous collapse. Her finger was already stabbing at the bell push to ring again.

"Hello, Mrs Portland," said Temple with concern. "Is anything wrong?"

She cast an apprehensive glance back down the stair-well. The lift was responding to a call from street level.

"Yes, I've got to talk to you. Now – before it's too late."

Without invitation she pushed past him into the hall. He closed the door behind her.

"What's happened?"

"I want to tell you why Moira committed suicide," she said rapidly. "I want you to know what she told me yesterday afternoon. I want to tell you about Madison. Now – before it's too late!"

8　Introducing Madison

Hearing Stella Portland's voice Steve had come out into the hall. She was shocked by Stella's appearance. It was as if invisible threads supporting her facial features had snapped. Her cheeks had sagged and a maze of lines had appeared round her eyes and mouth. Her eyes were red rimmed in an unnaturally pale face.

Solicitously Steve took her into the drawing-room and sat her down.

"You're not at all well, Mrs Portland. Would you like something to drink, a cup of tea?"

"No thanks. Just a glass of water."

Temple went to the drinks cabinet and poured her a glass of Malvern water. He and Steve watched anxiously while she drank it.

"That's better," she said, putting the glass down. "I've been so upset about Moira. It came as a great shock. You see, I was talking to her just before she – committed suicide."

Temple pulled a chair forward to sit down opposite her. "What did she tell you, Mrs Portland?"

"Well, as I told you, I saw her yesterday afternoon. The poor girl was obviously on the verge of a nervous breakdown. She told me the whole story – about herself and Sam and Chris Boyer."

"The whole story?"

"Well, you know the story about Sam, about his loss of memory and how he was discovered wandering down Portland Avenue in Chicago."

"Yes."

"For years he tried to discover his true identity. It was almost an obsession with him. He told you the story of the penny?"

"Yes, he did."

"He attached great importance to that penny, Mr Temple. Some months ago, Chris Boyer told Moira that he'd discovered Sam's identity. That he was the son of a man called Clint Dawson."

149

"Clint Dawson?"

"Yes. Dawson was a bogus company promoter. He swindled a lot of people out of their savings before the Fraud Squad caught up with him. He was sent to prison in 1949. Sam left England with his mother soon after that and no one knew where they went or what happened to them. It's pretty obvious now, of course, that they went to the States."

Stella glanced at Steve, who had sat down near her.

"Go on," prompted Temple.

"Chris discovered letters which were written by Dawson to his wife in which he mentions the penny. When Chris told Moira this story she asked him not to tell anyone because it might have drastic repercussions on the Portland Yeast Company."

"But why should it do that?" Steve asked.

"Well – if it became known that the head of the Company was the son of a swindler, then . . . "

"Like father like son?" Temple suggested.

Stella looked non-plussed. The saying meant nothing to her.

"Go on, Mrs Portland."

"Then Boyer started to blackmail her. He must have had thousands out of the poor girl. In the end Moira could stand it no longer and she told Boyer to send for her father and tell him the whole story. You know what happened . . . "

"Tell me."

"Boyer pretended that a private investigator called Madison discovered Sam's identity and he telexed for Sam to come over here. He put Hubert Greene's name to the telex because he realised that Sam would take more notice of it. If Sam hadn't died I believe that Boyer would have told him the whole story and then blackmailed him."

"Do you think Boyer really *did* discover the identity of your husband or was he just bluffing?"

"No. From what Moira told me, I'm pretty sure he was on to something. You see, Sam was right, that particular penny was an important link. If Boyer could have got hold of it he could have proved that Sam was the son of the notorious Dawson."

"Is that why the penny was changed?"

"Yes."

"Who changed it?"

"Moira did. She was determined that the penny shouldn't fall into the wrong hands. So she changed the 1923 penny for a 1957 one."

"Where is it now — the actual penny that Sam carried about with him?"

"It's here — I got it from Moira yesterday afternoon."

Stella dipped into her handbag and produced an envelope from which she extracted the coin.

"1923," said Paul, examining the 'tails' side. "Well, the date's all right anyway, Portland could certainly have had this penny in his pocket when he was arrested in 1952 — but that doesn't prove that this is the penny."

"There's an inscription. It's very, very faint, but if you look closely you can just see it."

Temple rose and took the penny over to the table lamp. "'To my son'," he read out. "'Good luck'. Then there are two initials. The first is C but I can't make out whether the second is a B or a D."

"Well I always thought it was a B and so did Sam, but if Boyer's story is true, then . . . "

"C.D.!" Steve exclaimed "Clint Dawson. Paul, the coin must have been given to Portland by his father."

"1923," said Stella thoughtfully. "That's probably the year that Sam was born — he always reckoned he was about sixty-four or five."

Temple was still staring at the coin, tilting it so that it reflected the light. He seemed to be willing it to tell him something.

"It seems to me, Mrs Portland," said Steve, "that you know everything there is to know about Boyer without having so much as a shred of evidence."

"I know. And that's the most dreadful part of the whole business. Unless, of course, your husband . . . " Stella looked up appealingly at Temple.

"Unless what, Mrs Portland?" Temple answered, with a faint smile.

"Unless you've got the evidence, Mr Temple?"

Temple handed the penny back to her. "I know the identity of Madison, Mrs Portland, and I've got quite enough evidence to arrest the gentleman — when the time comes."

Forbes' 'phone call had come through at three o'clock, just an hour after Stella Portland had left the flat. Two of Chief Inspector James' detectives had located the cottage at Lockdale. Forbes and James were already on their way down there. Could Temple meet them at Graveney Lock, on the Thames about seven miles upstream from Windsor?

Temple had rapidly picked out the relevant sheet from his set of 1:50 000 Ordnance Survey maps, had pin-pointed the lock and the approach road to it. Traffic had not yet built up to the evening rush-hour. He was able to make good time out of London and down the M4.

It was not yet four o'clock when the XJS nosed down the lane leading to a twelfth-century church which he had chosen as a reference point. The lane gave out three hundred yards from the river. Temple knew he was on the right track when he saw the police Rover parked near the church. The driver was sitting behind the wheel listening to the scenario of voices on his radio.

"About five minutes ago," he said, in answer to Temple's question. "They went along that path."

Temple broke into a ground-covering run and in less than a minute had reached the river.

Forbes and James were just being helped aboard a launch. It was moored to the bank a little way above the lock and its engines were running.

"Sorry to have kept you waiting," Temple apologised, a shade out of breath.

"We were just saying how quick you've been," said Forbes "It's only just gone four."

"So you finally found the cottage, James?"

"One of my men found it," said James laconically. "There was a message for me when I got back to the Yard."

The launch rocked as Temple jumped aboard.

"Was it at Lockdale?"

"Yes, but no wonder we couldn't spot it. It was built on the site of what must have been a country mansion. A run-down bungalow more than a cottage really. The Madison outfit have been using the cellar."

"Is it deserted?"

"It's derelict—you wouldn't look twice at the place."

"What's the cellar like?"

"You've never seen anything like it, Temple." Forbes was keeping his balance by holding on to the roof of the cabin. "And talk about equipment."

"It's an eye-opener," James confirmed. "No wonder they've been able to flood the Continent with counterfeit dollars."

"How long will it take us to get there?" Temple asked, as the launch headed out into the fast-flowing stream.

"Are you in a hurry?"

"I want to be back by eight at the latest."

"Oh, that's no problem," said Forbes.

The launch made good speed through the water, but the banks seemed to be going past much slower. It was a good half hour before they rounded a bend and saw a private mooring place where a cabin cruiser was already tied up. A burly, bare-headed figure in plain clothes standing beside it raised a hand in a minimal salute and James waved back. The launch veered into the landing place and the beat of the engine died.

"Afternoon, Sergeant," James greeted his detective cheerfully.

"Good afternoon, sir." Then, as Forbes stood up, the sergeant realised that the top brass was in on this. His body stiffened respectfully. "Oh, good afternoon, Sir Graham."

"Good afternoon, Sergeant."

"Anything to report?" James was reaching for the hand that was held out to help him ashore.

"Yes sir. There's someone in the cottage. A young fellow came down the tow-path about five minutes ago and went in it. We let him carry on because we didn't want to arouse his suspicions."

"What was he like – this young fellow?"

"Tall, dark, good looking, clean-shaven. Early thirties, I'd say, six foot tall and about a hundred and seventy pounds."

"Is he in the cottage now?"

"He's either there or in the cellar."

"Well done, Sergeant," said Forbes. Assisted by James he stepped up on to the bank, then reached back to give Temple a hand. "Come along, Temple. This could be interesting."

The 'cottage' lay several hundred yards back from the river and was surrounded by trees. From the river it was approached by a muddy path on to which brambles were enroaching. As they approached, a selection of exotic trees showed that this had once been a property of distinction. The building which now stood on the site of the old manor house looked like somebody's misguided attempt at a weekend refuge. How it had escaped the planning authority's eye was anybody's guess.

A second detective materialised from the trees as the group approached. He confirmed that the young man was still in the cottage. He had to be alone as no one else had entered the place either from the river or the pot-holed lane that led up to it from the main road.

"You watch the back of the house, Marsden," James told his man. "Sergeant Adams, keep an eye on the path and make sure no one disturbs us."

"Very good, sir."

Forbes and Temple followed James as he walked quietly up the grassy path that led to the door of the small building. Beside it stood an old-fashioned well with a thatched shelter and a bucket and chain for drawing up water. From a tree overhead a wood-pigeon took flight with an excessively loud clapping of its wings.

James tried the old-fashioned latch on the door.

"Seems to be locked," he muttered.

"Can I try?" said Temple. "We had a cottage like this once."

It required a strong pull on the door and considerable strength of hand to press the latch down silently. Then Temple exerted pressure with his foot at the same time as with his hand. The door opened with a faint creak.

The room onto which it gave was bare and dark. Only fingers of light filtered through the grimy, cob-webbed windows. Temple followed the swing of the door and entered. Forbes and James were at his back.

He could dimly see the figure standing in the middle of the room, but oddly he felt no threat from it.

"Good afternoon, Boyer."

"My God!" said Boyer. "You gave me a fright, Temple." He was trying to focus on Forbes and James against the sudden dazzle of light. "What is this? What are you doing here?"

"May one ask what you are doing here?"

"I had an appointment to meet someone here at five o'clock," said Boyer. "I was supposed to pick up a suitcase for Kelly. He told me he'd taken the cottage for weekends but I didn't expect it to be like this."

"There was no one here when you came?" demanded Forbes.

"No. I haven't seen anybody."

"But you found the suitcase," James pointed out.

Boyer slightly raised the suitcase he was carrying in his left hand. It was obviously heavy. "Yes. It was just standing in the middle of the room."

Forbes asked, "Do you know what's in it?"

"Oh, just books and papers," said Boyer vaguely. "That's what Kelly told me anyway."

"You haven't looked inside it?"

"No. It's locked."

Temple had moved round so that his shadow did not fall on the suitcase. He could just distinguish the maker's name. Samsonite.

He checked his watch. It was three minutes to five.

"Boyer!" The sharpness of his tone cut across James' question. "Your appointment here was for what time?"

"Five o'clock, Kelly said. On the dot."

"Excuse me." Temple took a pace towards Boyer and wrenched the suitcase from him.

"I say," Boyer protested. "Do you mind . . . "

But Temple was already at the door. With quick strides he covered the dozen yards to the old well. He swung the suitcase up and dropped it down the aperture. After a moment the sound of a heavy splash echoed up.

Boyer, James and Forbes were crowding at the door of the cottage.

"Get back inside!" Temple called as he ran towards them.

Something in his manner did not invite questions. The three men drew back inside the house. Temple, close behind them, slammed the door shut.

"Temple!" babbled Boyer. "You don't know what you've done."

"Don't I?" Temple retorted. "Stay away from those windows!"

Before he had time to check his watch there came from outside the sound of a heavy explosion. The building and the ground it stood on shook. The ancient glass of the windows fell out with a crash.

Forbes and James had instinctively ducked. Boyer had been punched to the floor by the blast.

"God!" he said, as he picked himself up. "What the hell was in that suitcase?"

"Well," said Temple. "It wasn't books."

"What time is it, Paul?"

"It's just gone half past eight."

"I don't know why but I feel awfully tired."

"Well, if you feel tired I should go to bed."

"I've a jolly good mind to."

"Did you finish your drink?"

"Yes."

"Like another?"

"No." Steve yawned hugely. "No, I don't think so. You know, I feel terribly sleepy."

"I expect you've been overdoing things, Steve. I should go and lie down."

"Charlie's making the most of your invitation to take the day off. He hasn't come in yet. I'm afraid if you want anything you'll have to get it for yourself."

"All right, darling," said Temple, sitting down with the evening paper.

But Steve still dallied, in spite of his obvious hints that he wanted to be left alone.

"Paul, what happened this afternoon at Lockdale?"

"I thought you said you were feeling off-colour. Go and lie down, Steve."

"Yes, all right." Steve yawned again. "Gosh I'm sleepy! It's funny I should feel like this. Goodnight, darling."

Temple had time to browse through the whole paper before his visitor arrived. He had heard the immersion heater humming and guessed that Steve was running a bath. There had been a shower of rain and the swish of car tyres on the King's Road was clearly audible. In the square an occasional door banged as some resident parked a car, and then the street became quiet again.

It was exactly nine o'clock when the front door buzzer sounded. Temple refolded his paper, got up and went quietly to open the door.

"Ah, hello, Greene. I've been expecting you. Come in."

"I hope I'm not too early," said Hubert Greene affably.

"No, you're in nice time. Shall I take your coat?"

"Thanks."

Greene took off his light shower-proof check coat. Underneath he was wearing a double-breasted pin-striped suit, very well padded round the shoulders.

Temple hung the coat up on a hanger and indicated the half-open door of his study. "Let's go into the study."

The desk light was on. Greene looked at the furniture, bookshelves and pictures admiringly.

"This is a very pleasant room."

"Yes, it is rather." Temple agreed. "Would you like a drink?"

"Well – er . . . "

"I'm having a whisky and soda."

"Oh, well, thanks." Greene moved to the rug in front of the fireplace while Temple poured him a generous drink. "I say, it was very odd about that note, wasn't it?"

"Yes, wasn't it?"

"I can't imagine why anyone else should send it."

"May I see it?"

"Yes, of course, I've brought it for you."

Greene withdrew a folded A4 sheet from his inside pocket and handed it to Temple. The message was type-written. Temple unfolded it and read it aloud.

"Dear Mr Greene,
  I should be grateful if you would call round and see me this
   morning at twelve o'clock.
Yours sincerely,
Paul Temple."

Temple looked up to ask, "Did you call round this morning?"

"No, I told you on the 'phone I was detained at the office, I couldn't make it."

"Yes, of course," Temple murmured with a nod.

"Temple, who *did* send this note?" Greene demanded, riled by Temple's casual manner.

"Don't you know? It was Sir Graham."

"Sir Graham! Are you joking?"

"No."

"But why should Sir Graham send it?" Greene was really puzzled now.

"Because I asked him to."

"Because you . . ." Two vertical lines of anger had appeared between Greene's brows. "Look here, Temple, what is this?"

"I asked Sir Graham to send you a note because I wanted you to call round at twelve o'clock this morning."

"But why didn't you write the note yourself?"

"Well, if I'd written it myself I couldn't truthfully have said that I hadn't written it, could I?" Temple was still talking in a calm and reasonable tone, as if he was explaining something to a very simple child. "And if I couldn't have said that I hadn't written it, you wouldn't be here."

"I may be dense but I'm afraid I don't follow you."

"Don't you? It's really quite simple. You came here this evening because you were quite genuinely puzzled about the note. If you hadn't been puzzled you wouldn't have come. That's true, isn't it?"

"Yes, but – do you mean to say the note was a hoax to get me here this evening?"

"No," said Temple with a smile, "to get you here this morning – at twelve o'clock."

"But I didn't come here this morning," Greene protested.

"I'm sorry to contradict you, but you did."

Greene had paled. The expression in his eyes was dangerous. "If I say I didn't come then I didn't come."

Temple's only change of expression was to raise an eyebrow. He folded the typewritten message and put it in his own pocket. Then he picked up his glass, took a sip and contemplated Greene over the rim. The friendliness had suddenly gone from his manner.

"Greene, I think it's time you realised I know what your game is."

"What the hell do you mean?" Greene was still staring angrily at Temple.

"For quite a while now," said Temple quietly, holding Greene's eyes with his own, "I've suspected that you were Madison, that you were the brains behind the counterfeit racket. You were also responsible for the murder of Chunky Brooks and of your own wife, Eileen. You also killed Dordrecht and Elzec, you very nearly killed Kelly and you are answerable for the deaths of one policeman and a crew member in that river explosion. Let me tell you something, Greene," Temple's voice was still quiet and unemotional but there was a hint of the whip-lash in it now, "I've met a great many criminals in my time, but I don't think I've ever met one quite as vicious as you. If you'd stuck to the counterfeit racket you might have got away with it. Unfortunately you went in for blackmail as well."

"Oh, I'm supposed to be a blackmailer as well, am I?" Greene had recovered sufficiently to bring a note of sarcasm into his voice. "My word, I do sound an unpleasant customer! Just as a matter of interest, who am I supposed to have blackmailed?"

"You blackmailed Mrs Portland into telling me a very interesting story – a perfectly true story, except for one important detail. It was you, and *not* Chris Boyer, who discovered that Sam Portland was the son of a swindler. It was you, and *not* Boyer, who blackmailed Moira. When she refused to be blackmailed any longer you sent for Sam. When Sam died you tried to get hold of the penny to substantiate your story. You knew that if you had the penny you could go on blackmailing and eventually gain control of the Portland Yeast Company."

"This is a most interesting story." Greene was now pretending to be mildly amused. "Tell me, it's a small point, but why am I supposed to have murdered Chunky Brooks?"

"Because you knew that he was receiving information from one of your people, Mark Kendell. But that was when you made your first mistake. You left a penny at the scene of Chunky's murder. That was intended to make us think his death was connected with the Madison mystery. But your penny was the wrong date. It should have been 1923, not 1952."

Greene was still composed but the colour had drained from his face.

"And are you accusing me of killing my own wife?"

"I am. You knew she had found out about the counterfeit set-up and was in contact with a CID man. Brooks asked her to find out about the movements of couriers. Unfortunately – fatally, in fact – she gave herself away."

"So I – just eliminated her?" said Greene, with an incredulous laugh.

"So you just eliminated her," Temple agreed seriously. "Doing your best, of course, to throw suspicion on Kelly. But Kelly had seen you going down to the boat-house with Eileen that night. He threw the knife at our door in a desperate attempt to get help to her in time and then when he realised he was being set up as Eileen's killer he made a pathetic attempt to throw dust in our eyes by claiming he had found the diamond clip . . . "

"You know, Temple, I can understand why your books are so successful—"

"You decided Kelly was expendable," Temple went on remorselessly. "You sent him to the cottage at Lockdale to pick up a suitcase. But Kelly outsmarted you there. He sent Boyer instead, telling him that the suitcase contained counterfeit notes and that if he played along Madison would cut him in on the racket . . . "

The rug had become scuffed up under Greene's feet. He waved a hand at the shelves of books.

"If the stories under those covers are half as good as the one you're inventing now—."

Once again Temple did not let him finish. He moved behind his desk, which faced outwards across the room from a corner, and looked down at his 'phone and ansaphone.

"You're clever with electronics, aren't you? Time fuses and radio-activated explosives and that sort of thing. So you know how easy it is to bug a telephone."

Greene was like a man turned to stone. Only his eyes moved as he worked out the implications of what Temple had said.

"So that was it," he almost whispered. "You bugged the 'phone and rigged the ansaphone to record our conversation."

"Exactly." Temple's hand moved to lift the telephone

receiver. "Like to see how it works? Of course the cassette's been removed . . . "

"*Don't touch that 'phone!*" Greene commanded harshly. His hand had delved inside that well padded left shoulder. It came out holding a stubby black automatic. He pointed it unwaveringly at Temple's midriff.

Temple arrested the movement of his hand. He measured the distance between himself and Greene with his eye.

"Greene, I think you ought to know that there are three men watching the house and a fourth on the lift, so if you have any melodramatic ideas . . . "

"Behold!" said Greene, "I have a weapon . . . "

"By Timothy!" Temple breathed, staring at the man. He had declaimed the line as if acting his part in a play.

"There's an important point, Temple, which you appear to have overlooked."

"Oh, yes?" said Temple, playing for time. He knew now that he was dealing with someone whose mind was unhinged. Strangely he felt no sense of personal danger.

"You claim to be able to read my mind, so you must know that I have not the slightest intention of being arrested and left to rot for the rest of my life in some stinking gaol. So I have nothing to lose by killing you. Turn round and put your hands against that wall behind . . . "

Before Temple had time to obey, the door opened. Steve was still fully dressed. She stood there, taking in the scene – Temple behind his desk apparently calm. Greene, grasping the automatic and looking as wild and unpredictable as a jackal. The gun had swung to cover her.

"One move, Temple, and she gets it. Come in, Mrs Temple. Stand beside your husband."

"Do as he says, Steve," Temple told her.

Steve, mesmerised by Greene's threatening crouch, came round the open door and stood beside her husband. His apparent unconcern reassured her a little.

"Now, turn round, both of you, and place your hands against the wall."

Temple obeyed and Steve followed suit. It was a replay of the scene in the bedroom when Mark Kendell had broken in. But Greene was wilier than the man he had trained. He kept his distance as he moved towards the door.

"Now, don't imagine I won't use this thing," he threatened again. "Keep your head down, Temple."

Temple heard the quick swish of his feet across the carpet, heard the key being taken out of the door and inserted on the outside, heard the door slam and the key turn. A moment later came the sound of the front door being closed quietly.

By then he and Steve had lowered their arms and turned round.

"Steve, I thought you'd gone to bed . . . "

"I know you did," retorted Steve drily. "Did you think I couldn't tell that you'd doctored my drink? It was obvious you were up to something. What are we going to do now? He's locked us in."

For answer, Temple opened the top drawer of his desk and took out the spare key he had put there. He was banking on Greene having extracted the key of the study door before leaving the flat.

He had. Temple was able to insert the key and turn it.

As he went out into the hall he saw that in his haste Greene had bequeathed them his check shower-proof overcoat.

A key was already scraping in the lock of the front door. It opened to reveal the alarmed face of Charlie, returning from a day with his pals in Stepney. He stared wide-eyed at Paul and Steve.

"Blimey, what's going on here?"

Temple had seen that the lift was already ascending from the ground floor. "Did you see Mr Greene?"

"Greene? Was that the bloke in the grey suit and . . . "

"Yes," snapped Temple impatiently. "Did you see him?"

" 'Course I saw him. Blimey, he wasn't 'alf in a hurry. He ran upstairs like a scalded cat."

"Upstairs?"

"S'right."

"Are you sure?"

" 'Course I'm sure."

The lift had come level with the third floor landing. The door opened and Detective Chief Inspector James stepped out.

"What's happened, Temple?"

162

"He's made a dash for it, James – he's gone upstairs. Is Sir Graham with you?"

"He's in the car outside. Is there an exit up there?"

"There's a fire-escape from the roof into a cul-de-sac."

"Where's the cul-de-sac – at the back of the building?"

"Yes, I'll show you . . . "

"Paul!" Steve had seized Paul's arm. "Leave it to the police. I think I may be going to faint . . . "

"Oh, my God!" said Temple with concern. He took her arm and as James pulled his radio set out to warn his men that Greene had gone over the roofs, he led her back into the flat. He did not see the look she gave Charlie.

"It looks as if he's beaten us, Temple."

"Not yet, Sir Graham. I think I know where he'll head for."

A quarter of an hour had passed since Greene had disappeared on to the roof. A dozen policemen had scoured the block and the mews behind it, their search co-ordinated by pocket radios. Forbes and James were forced to admit that Greene had slipped from their net.

The two CID men were standing in the hall of the Temples' flat with Temple and Steve. Sounds of bumping still came from the roof two floors overhead.

"You know where he's heading?" echoed James sceptically.

"Yes. He'll make for 'Brown Acres'."

"Brown Acres?" said Forbes, trying to read Temple's expression. "What makes you think that?"

"Something he said when he pulled the gun on me. If we move fast we can get there before he does."

Forbes hesitated for only a moment.

"Right," he said. "Let's get moving. You'll come too, Temple?"

"But, Sir Graham," James objected. "We've no good reason for believing . . . "

"That's my decision, James," Forbes snapped. "You can leave half a dozen men here in case he shows up. We're going down to 'Brown Acres'."

It was a squash for the four of them to fit into the car as well as the driver. Temple had realised that Steve was on his heels only when he reached the street. Her faintness had miraculously passed. Rather than argue the point he

163

accepted the inevitable. She slipped into the back seat where she was wedged between her husband and Sir Graham. James sat in front beside the driver. Temple noted with satisfaction that he was the same young man as had driven them down to Windsor on the night they had rescued Steve.

As soon as the doors were closed and seat-belts snapped home the driver let in his clutch. Forbes had authorised the use of the flashing blue light and the siren. Drivers checked and heads turned as the police car swung out into King's Road and headed west.

Temple grabbed the support strap as the Rover rocked through Sloane Square and then on down the King's Road.

"I'll go over Putney Bridge, sir," the driver said, changing up one gear, "and pick up the Kingston by-pass."

"Whichever's quickest," gasped James, closing his eyes as the car squeezed between a bus and a lorry. He turned in his seat, the radio mike in his hand. "I'll alert all cars in the Leatherhead area, Sir Graham. We can seal 'Brown Acres' off."

"Sir Graham," said Temple. "We don't want any police cars near the place till we know Greene is there. That's vitally important."

"We'll do it Temple's way," Sir Graham told the Chief Inspector.

James' expression showed clearly what he thought as he faced forward again.

"Paul," said Steve, "I realise now that Greene is Madison, but there's an awful lot I don't understand. What made you suspect him in the first place?"

"Didn't you suspect him? Hubert Greene is an extraordinary character. I realised that the first time I met him at Southampton. Then there was that night at the Manila when he persuaded Moira to go down to his place for the weekend."

"Was that why he was at the Manila – to see Moira?"

"That was not the only reason. Elzec had told him that Mark Kendell was going to meet Archie Brooks there. Greene had already heard about him from Eileen and wanted to take a look—"

Temple's explanation was cut off as they were all thrown

forward. A small van had turned out of a side street in the path of the charging police car.

"Silly little man," was all the driver said, as he snicked into first gear and accelerated to 60 m.p.h.

"But why on earth did he invite us down to 'Brown Acres' for the weekend?"

"Greene was extraordinarily arrogant. He had already made up his mind to murder Eileen and throw suspicion onto Kelly. It gave him a perverse amusement to use us as witnesses to his innocence, but Kelly outsmarted him. At first I thought he'd killed his wife because she was informing Brooks about him. Now I think there was another reason, and a much more complex one."

"Was it Kelly who threw the knife at our bedroom door?"

"Yes."

"But how do you know?"

Temple glanced at Forbes, who was listening intently to this conversation.

"When Sam Portland died George Kelly was out of a job . . . "

"And a very soft job too," grunted Forbes.

" . . . Greene very quickly weighed up the situation. He told Kelly that if he co-operated with him he'd be taken care of. For a time Kelly did precisely what Greene told him . . . "

"Even to the extent of telephoning you at the Manila," Forbes chimed in again.

"I knew all along it was Kelly," commented Steve.

"But Kelly began to get too ambitious. He'd discovered that Greene was not only into blackmail but was also running the counterfeit racket. He wanted a part of that. Greene decided that he had to do something about Kelly. He made up his mind when he began to suspect that Kelly and Eileen were having an affair."

"And were they?"

"Who knows? But Eileen was an attractive and flirtatious woman and you saw that she and Greene had separate bedrooms. My own opinion is that Greene was insanely jealous – both of Brooks and Kelly."

The car was crossing Putney Bridge. The river gleamed briefly to left and right. Then they were in the crowded canyon of Putney High Street, the siren wailing non-stop and echoing from the blank windows of the shops. It was the slowest and most frustrating part of the journey, but one thing the driver had learnt at the Hendon Police School was to keep his cool. At last they were through the sludge of traffic and racing up Putney Hill. Once on the Kingston by-pass the car built up speed to 120 m.p.h.

"Paul, what was all that about this morning? First you give Charlie the day off and then you tell me to ring you from a call box with a story about . . . "

Temple had to raise his voice to be heard above the tyre and wind roar. "Let me explain, Steve. I asked Kelly to the flat and I also told Sir Graham to send Greene a note asking him to call in at twelve mid-day. As soon as Kelly arrived you telephoned, which was exactly what I wanted."

"In other words you left Kelly alone in the flat."

"Exactly. In my study, to be precise. And at twelve o'clock, bang on cue, Hubert Greene turned up. Kelly opened the door, as I had asked him and took Greene into my study."

"So that's why you wanted to know about telephone bugging, Temple," Forbes cut in.

"Yes. I hoped that if Greene and Kelly were left alone together some interesting things might emerge."

James had turned round so that he could hear better. Steve was squeezed even tighter between Temple and Sir Graham by the G forces as the driver turned left onto the A243. The traffic had thinned considerably.

"Switch the blue lights off, Foster," Forbes directed. "And we won't use the siren from now on."

"Very good, sir," replied Foster, just a little disappointed.

"And did you?" Forbes asked.

"Did I what?"

"Learn anything interesting."

"I certainly did – at least when I had a chance to listen to the tape." Temple chuckled. "There's not much love lost between those two."

"Excuse me, sir," interrupted Foster, his eyes not leaving the road. "Do I take the by-pass for Dorking?"

"No," Temple told him. "Go through the town. I'll give you the route. We're nearly there, I'd better make this brief. First, I heard Greene trying to justify killing Eileen and admitting he tried to throw suspicion on Kelly. It's tantamount to a confession. Kelly was genuinely fond of Eileen, throwing the knife at our door was a desperate attempt to get help to her in time . . . "

"Was he a witness to the murder?" James asked.

"No, but he'd seen Greene walking her down to the boathouse. Secondly . . . " Temple was ticking the points off on his fingers. "I had confirmation that it was Greene who killed Elzec. When he bumped into Kelly coming out of the lift he thought it was me . . . "

"Oh, Paul!" Steve winced as she remembered the condition of Kelly's face.

"Anyway, Kelly thought he had enough on Greene to do a little blackmailing on his own account. He persuaded Greene to supply him with fifty thousand pounds and an air passage to New York. Greene told him that the money would be waiting for him in a suitcase at Lockdale. He only had to go there and pick it up. But Kelly smelt a rat. He sent Boyer instead with a story that Madison was going to cut him in on the counterfeit racket."

"All this is on the tape?"

"Yes, Sir Graham. And Hubert Greene realised it. That's why he pulled the gun on me. If Steve hadn't come in . . . "

"Well," said James with satisfaction. "Mr Kelly will not be flying to New York. We picked him up at Heathrow this evening."

"I don't know why, Paul, but I feel rather sorry about that. I was quite fond of Kelly."

"Yes," said Temple, "he did have a way with the ladies."

"You said there was another reason why Greene killed his wife." The lights of an oncoming car shed a pale illumination on Steve's face. Ahead the street lamps of Leatherhead had come into view. "What did you mean by that?"

Temple was leaning forward to be ready to direct the driver.

"How well do you know your *Othello*, Steve?"

"I know he murdered his wife out of jealousy, but she was innocent."

"And then?" Temple prompted. But when she was lost for a reply he leant forward to be ready to direct the driver through Leatherhead and out onto the minor road that led to 'Brown Acres'.

"I hope we're here before Greene," remarked Forbes.

"If he comes at all," rejoined Chief Inspector James drily. "I wish we'd got the place properly staked out."

"It'll be all right," Temple assured him. "The fewer there are of us the better. Another three hundred yards, Foster. The gates are on the left. Can you see with sidelights?"

The driver slowed and switched off his headlamps. There was diffused moonlight seeping through a thin layer of clouds. The wrought iron gates were just discernible as a break in the wall. The driver swung in, using a high gear to reduce noise. The sidelights showed up only the boles of the trees lining the avenue. By the time they reached the lake the three men's eyes had grown accustomed to the dark. They could see its surface gleaming dully as the car glided past.

Then the house came in view, standing at the top of the slope. Its windows were in total darkness. There was no sign of any car on the driveway.

Still at Temple's suggestion the police car was parked out of sight under an ancient yew tree behind the house. Forbes and James took up position on a level with the front steps. A sheltered bench made them invisible to anyone coming up the drive, but no one could enter the house without being seen by them.

Temple had decided that he would keep watch down at the boat-house. Steve had categorically refused to be separated from him. James was not happy about the situation at all and kept muttering about the dozen police marksmen he would have deployed as a reception commit-tee for Greene.

"Have you a gun?" Steve asked as they went down the path towards the lake.

"Yes, but I shan't need it. Don't talk any more, just in case he's here already."

Steve put her arm into Paul's. Her shivering was as much fright as cold. She simply could not understand why he was prepared to expose himself in this way.

The moonlight was stronger now and the surface of the lake had a lambent sheen. The silence was absolute, no birds stirred at the water's edge and even the lapping of waves was stilled.

They followed the path round the lake's edge, going in the opposite direction to that walk they had taken the afternoon they had been Hubert Greene's guests. They were walking in the footsteps of George Kelly when he had tried to plant the bogus evidence of the diamond clip, and in the footsteps of Greene as he had led his wife to her death.

Temple freed his arm from Steve as they approached the boat-house. He stood for several minutes, just listening, before he approached it.

The boat lay silently inside, its oars shipped, the blades dry.

"We're on time," he whispered.

"What do we do now?" she breathed in reply.

"We climb up there and wait."

There was a ladder giving access to the space below the pitched roof, which was used as a store for boating gear. Temple went first and then helped Steve up. The roof space gave cover from rain but the gable at each end was open. They looked down onto the path at one end and overlooked the lake at the other. At the same time Temple could watch the door to the boat-house through the hatch they had come up by.

They made themselves reasonably comfortable on tarpaulins and boat cushions and settled down to wait. The silence closed around them and they began to pick up tiny noises that had been inaudible before – the gentle stirring of the boat, a tiny creature rustling dry leaves, the pad of a night predator stalking its prey.

The loudest sound was the clock in the tower of a nearby church. They heard it strike 11 . . . 11.15 . . . 11.30 . . .

Temple was waiting for the quarter before midnight to strike when he saw the brief flash of a torch. Someone was on the path, approaching from the opposite direction.

Greene must have left whatever vehicle he had come in near the entrance to the avenue.

Temple squeezed Steve's arm to warn her. He held his breath and peered through the hatch.

The first sound he heard was Greene's breathing, the quick breathing of a man under stress. Then a shadow flitted across his field of vision.

Greene was below them in the boat-house.

They could hear his movements as he untied the painter, stepped shakily into the boat, took up an oar to push it out onto the lake. Interspersed with the panting were incoherent mutterings. "I kissed the . . . I kissed the . . . "

"Paul," Steve whispered. "What's he . . . "

"Sh."

Greene was using an oar and a hand to propel the boat out onto the lake. A short jetty protruded twelve feet beyond the boat-house. When he was clear of that, he fitted both oars into the rowlocks, began to pull for the open water. The thump of the oars on the gunwales and the splash of the blades in the water carried clearly across the water. From up at the house came the grunt of a voice, then footsteps on the gravel.

"Damn!" Temple uncoiled his legs. He began to climb down the ladder. "No, Steve, you stay up here."

He had reached the small jetty when suddenly the whole lake was illuminated by two sets of car headlamps. One pair of beams was coming up from near the house, the other from half way along the avenue. They transfixed Greene with a light as if on a double spit.

"Greene!" James' voice boomed out, amplified by a loud hailer. "You are surrounded. Throw your weapon into the stern of the boat."

Greene had stopped rowing. He let the oars flop into the water. Slowly and unsteadily he rose to his feet. The smart, double-breasted grey suit gleaming in the white light was eerily incongruous.

Then Greene reached into the shoulder holster. He pulled out the black automatic. The metal sent out glinting reflections.

Temple called out, "Greene!" Greene swung to face this new threat. Temple was etched as clearly as he was by the merciless light. "Don't do it."

"Is that Temple?"

"Yes. Throw the gun down like he said."

For answer, Greene seized the automatic with both hands in a marksman's grip. He raised it high and then brought it down pointing at Temple. Dazzled by the light, all Temple could hear was the sound of feet running down the path from the house.

"Temple?"

"Yes."

" 'An honourable murderer' if you like."

Then Greene turned the automatic towards his head and fired. Behind him Temple heard Steve's scream of horror. He did not wait to see the body topple into the water. He dashed along the jetty towards his wife and caught her as she swayed with eyes tight closed.

Forbes and James found them three minutes later. Temple still holding Steve in his arms.

"You were right, Temple," Forbes exclaimed. "But why were you so sure he would come here?"

Temple slowly released Steve, making sure that she was steady on her feet.

"Greene had once been a Shakespearian actor. I realised he was identifying with Othello when he said, " 'Behold, I have a weapon'. I recognised the quotation. I knew then that he was bent on his own suicide. You heard his last words. That was a quote from Othello's speech before he kills himself."

"Yes, of course," said James. "I remember now!"

Steve had a worried look on her face as she gazed towards the empty boat, rocking on the lake. The first ripples had only just reached the opposite bank. Finally, she turned and looked at Temple. He smiled.

"A penny for your thoughts, Steve . . ."